T0158513

PLAYING THE POOLS

ALSO BY DAVID M. SINDALL

After Alyson
Snatched

PLAYING
THE
Pools

DAVID M. SINDALL

Red Door

Published by RedDoor
www.reddoorpress.co.uk

© 2021 David M. Sindall

ISBN 978-1-913062-48-4

A CIP catalogue record for this book is available from the British
Library

Cover design: Emily Courdelle

Typesetting: Jen Parker, Fuzzy Flamingo

Printed and bound in Denmark by Nørhaven

*For my Dad, my friends, and all of the other mad people who
have played for or supported Tranmere Rovers*

PART 1

'Everybody must have a fantasy'
Andy Warhol

PROLOGUE

The fluorescent light is too bright for the mood but sadly all too fit for purpose. The room is disturbingly quiet, save for the noise of the city's traffic, soft and droning, like some distant song. There are rows of steel drawers lining the walls, and it occurs to him that they must all house similarly gruesome contents. A medic in a white coat gestures him over, a little Indian man, with a gentle, sympathetic manner. He says a few words.

'We have had the body for about a week now. The features are a bit swollen. The right cheekbone has been injured, but the skin is not broken – just bruised...' He pauses, adding eye contact to his gentle commentary. 'We will now open the unit. You must nod when you are ready, and we will pull the sheet down to reveal the upper third of the torso. In the event of a positive identification, you don't need to say anything. Just nod your head *yes* or shake it *no*.' He demonstrates, as though he's introducing an entirely new concept of communication.

The drawer is pulled open, and he's already certain from the shape and size of the body that it's them. He feels sick. He feels hot tears ready to burst forth. He manages to keep it together, though. He's ready. He nods.

The sheet is pulled back; the body is face down. He looks to the left shoulder for no more than a second or two and sees a tattoo. It's a Tranmere Rovers crest, with the club's motto, 'Lux et Robur', indelibly marked on the yellowing skin.

He knows who this is. He nods again.

NEW YEAR'S DAY, 1963

This is brilliant, Reggie Kellison thinks as he glances around the room. *This is paradise!*

He's sitting in the most fantastic restaurant he's ever set foot in, and any minute now he'll be joined by Laura. He can sense the excitement mounting in his throat; the same feeling he used to get as a kid on Christmas Day.

Dressed in a white dinner suit and black bow tie, he really does think he looks the part. Diners at the other tables are looking across, smiling, giving admiring nods and glances. A magnum of champagne is presented to him.

'Your Bollinger, sir,' the waiter says, lifting the bottle from an ice bucket and removing the foil from its neck.

A loud pop follows, the drinks are poured and he hands a ten-shilling note to the departing flunky, who bows slightly in appreciation of the generous tip. Then, chilled glass in hand, he waits expectantly for Laura to join him, knowing that any moment now she'd appear at the top of the staircase. Every eye in the restaurant would follow her as they all wondered which table she was headed for, and then she'd glance up and wave her gloved hand in his direction, and everyone would know that she was with Reggie Kellison; she was his girl. After that, there'd be more admiring glances, and even more respect.

He takes a sip of his champagne, enjoying its taste and luxuriating in the indulgence, when, quite unexpectedly, an alarm starts ringing. It grows louder and louder, and soon the diners around him begin to lose their composure. Suddenly, they all disappear, along with the restaurant, melting into grey. He hears a woman's shouts, getting nearer and more familiar.

'Reggie – Reggie,' she calls. 'It's time to get up, Reg!'

He opens his eyes to darkness; the air around his ears is cold. Cath, his wife, nudges him, and sleepily she says, 'You'll miss the bus if you don't get up now.'

He wishes that he didn't have to get up, and that his head wasn't still a bit fuzzy after overindulging on New Year's Eve. However, he's agreed to do overtime today, and overtime means getting out of bed, swinging his legs down onto the lino, shaving in a freezing-cold bathroom and getting the 6.30a.m. bus to the ferry before catching another bus to Littlewoods Pools. It'll take him an hour if he's lucky, but longer if the bus is late. If his luck is out, he'll have to stand in the cold, on this coldest of January mornings, his hands freezing and his coat turned up against his neck, with his bollocks feeling like they're about to drop off.

It's no wonder then, given the circumstances, that he stays where he is, comforted by the warmth of the bed and the heat from his wife's body next to him. *So, this is 1963*, he thinks. *It feels very similar to 1962.*

He stares up at the ceiling and soon starts to feel guilty that he hasn't yet swung his legs out into the chill of the room. He's aware that in a few days' time, their sixth, and hopefully final, child will be born. He never intended to be a dad of six; he only ever wanted a couple of kids, but Cath was never happier than when her belly was swollen. If she wasn't preparing to give birth, she was either getting over a pregnancy or planning the next one. They'd been lucky with this one, after she almost

2

miscarried early on. As it turned out, she'd lost a twin, but the baby who survived seemed to be going to full term. It had been a massive relief, obviously, but there's still a part of him that wonders how they're going to keep it fed and clothed.

Finally, he summons the courage to get out of bed. His feet hit the icy lino, and his body spasms as the floor bites into his skin. He searches in the dark for his slippers, but they're nowhere to be found; either one of the kids has moved them, or he left them downstairs last night. As a result, he has to brave the bedroom floor, the landing and then the bathroom with his feet frozen solid underneath him.

While shaving, he wonders what it would feel like to do it in hot water, rather than the icy stuff that idles in the basin in front of him. The shock of the cold water has him fully awake at least, banishing his dreams to the part of his brain that will only become active again when his head hits the pillow that night. The extra few minutes in bed have cost him a warming cup of tea, and before he knows it, he's pulling on his coat and heading for the bus stop.

The journey is mostly a blur of sensory reactions. He shivers as he waits for his bus, and once on board he sits as near to the front as he can, absorbing what little warmth escapes from the heater behind the driver's cab. On the ferry crossing, he sits beneath deck, again seeking out the warmest corners for the short trip. As he comes up on deck, seeing the Liver Buildings and Pier Head, he has no sense that Liverpool is about to become the centre of the universe. He has a vague notion of who the Beatles are, but only because of his eldest son, Barry. As far as Reggie's concerned, the whole Merseybeat scene could be taking place on another continent. His life doesn't embrace the new. He doesn't have space for novelty or fads or fashion; he's a simple man trying to make his honest way in the world.

As his second bus makes its way from the city centre to Edge Lane, his thoughts are of Tranmere, Tranmere and Tranmere. *Music?* Music is just noise. Soon enough, he's standing before the grandeur of the Littlewoods building, ready to strip off his overcoat, hang it in his locker and face another day like every other day, checking to see whether or not he can help a poor man become rich. It's not the life he wants, and certainly not the life he envisaged, but it's the only life he has. He's not content, but nor is he unhappy.

Passing a mirror in the gents' toilets, he glances at the person staring back at him. He knows this isn't the face of a miserable man, but that it isn't a picture of satisfaction, either. What he sees in his reflection is discontent, soured by the bitterness of a life that has offered little sweetness. Instead, his lot comprises whinging kids, unfulfilled potential and a growing belief that he'll never ever realise his dreams.

He's at his desk now, the first to arrive. Soon, he'll be joined by the others, like Fred Hughes, his best mate at work, who has the desk next to him. Then there's Jeff Morris, or Lord Haw-Haw as he's known, a jumped-up, working-class Tory, who thinks he's a cut above the people around him. Bert Fosh, Peter Barlow and Jenny Taylor complete the team of six.

His musings are interrupted by the arrival of his supervisor, Mr Hurworth.

'Morning, Reggie,' he chimes. 'Happy New Year.'

Reggie greets Hurworth with a smile and a nod, thinking that he isn't a bad sort, really. He's fair and always tries to lead the team with an even hand. He's still a boss, though.

'Any news on the new arrival, Reg?'

'Any day now, Mr Hurworth. Cath's belly is big enough to block the Mersey Tunnel.'

'Only five more until you've got a starting eleven. In fact, if you were to take your whole family to Prenton Park, you'd

4

double the gate,' Hurworth laughs, indulging in his own joke.

Reggie chuckles politely. It's a weak line, but it was said without malice. He decides to take advantage of the office being quiet.

'Any news back from Mr Roberts?' he asks, hoping to get the new year off to a positive start.

'Not yet, Reggie, but if you want my opinion, it's a smashing idea. People don't like Aussie football, and they're much more likely to have an interest in cricket.'

At the start of December, Reggie had submitted an idea to management for a summer cricket pool. From May to mid-August, Littlewoods uses Australian football results while waiting for the new British football season to begin, and although this is enough to keep things ticking over, only around a third of the regular punters bother. This means that there's less work to do and less overtime, and people end up twiddling their thumbs or, worse, being placed on a four-day week during summer. With that in mind, a cricket pool seemed a no-brainer, since punters are much more likely to be interested in Lancashire or Middlesex than some obscure Australian football teams. The chances of winning would be slightly higher, but the permutations were much greater, so Reggie's convinced that this suggestion is a sure-fire winner.

He'd submitted the proposal as a long handwritten letter, having spent six weeks drafting and revising until he was finally confident that he'd got it spot on. Littlewoods has a policy of developing internal ideas and, over the years, a number of employees have received prize money of one thousand guineas as reward for their ingenuity. That would be enough to buy a decent house in Bebington or Oxton, and build a better life for him, Cathy and the kids.

His reverie is broken by Fred's noisy arrival.

'Alright, Reggie. Fucking freezing out there!'

Reggie laughs at Fred's crudeness. He isn't one for swearing himself, but he doesn't mind indulging Fred.

'Mr Hughes, could you moderate your language, please?' Hurworth says, giving Fred a look of distaste. 'Fortunately, the ladies have yet to arrive, otherwise I might have to be more forceful with you.'

'I'm sorry, Mr Hurworth,' Fred says. 'It's just so friggin' cold, isn't it?'

'Mr Hughes, may I suggest that you don't consider a career as a weather forecaster. Not only do you lack the verbal acuity, but also, I think you'll find that the weather is more or less as it should be at this time of the year.'

Reggie has always liked the fact that Mr Hurworth uses intellect, rather than bullying, to pull Fred into line. To him, Hurworth is like a good football manager, knowing exactly how to prod and push in order to get the best from his players. He also likes how Fred doesn't seem to care one iota. He just carries on spluttering away, oblivious to the insults.

'Right you are, Mr Hurworth,' Fred says and then turns to Reggie and mouths, 'Fuckwit!'

Reggie forces a cough to cover a giggle, just as Morris walks into the office.

'Lord Haw-Haw!' Fred shouts. 'Did you enjoy your Christmas at Sandringham, wiping the backsides of the Windsors?'

'Hughes, you're such a pleb,' Morris answers dismissively.

'What, didn't you even get an invite?' Reggie joins in. 'Nice Wirral Grammar lad like you?'

Morris ignores Reggie, focusing his ire on Fred. 'And what are your New Year's resolutions, Hughes? To stop drinking out of the toilet bowl? To learn to hold a knife and fork?'

'Oh, stop it, Haw-Haw, my sides are splitting,' Fred says sarcastically. 'We're supposed to be funny, us Scousers. You might want to look that up in a book called the dictionary. Get your butler to fetch it for you when you get home to Haw-Haw Towers tonight.'

Their slanging match stops when Jenny enters the office. The verdict on Jenny is that she's a 'lovely' girl, which, truth be told, was a code word for saying that she was fat. Her favourite pastimes are dreaming about getting married and eating cream cakes, but she doesn't seem to realise that the chances of the first are greatly reduced by the regularity of the second. When she first started at Littlewoods, she was a curvy, Marilyn Monroe-esque size 14, but she's now closer to a Hattie Jacques 18. She still has a pretty face, but her beauty has become like a green belt field with new housing added: still pleasant, but not as aesthetically pleasing as it used to be.

To complete the team, Peter Barlow, AKA the Corpse, arrives. This nickname is on account of him never being on time, making him 'the late Peter Barlow'. Not much is known about Pete, as a result of the fact that once he's in, he spends most of the day trying to make up for lost time. He's often reluctant to make the tea, which is a pity, as the general consensus is that the Corpse makes the best tea out of all of them.

'Right, team,' Hurworth pipes up. 'We've got the remainder of the third dividends to track down today. Let's see if we can get it cracked by four o'clock. If we can, I'll buy you all a drink to celebrate the New Year when we finish at five.'

The offer is met with murmurs of approval, and the team quickly warms to the task. The world of football pools is complex to the outsider. A first dividend win requires the correct prediction of eight score draws on a week when those are the only eight games out of a possible forty-eight that meet the criteria. Any punter lucky enough to win on a first divi week would rake in a sum in excess of a hundred thousand, so there was always a sense of excitement whenever one came around. However, the previous week had seen eleven score draws, meaning that the payout would be smaller. The team is tasked with trawling through the orders they processed to check that no customers have missed out on a small win, which in the case of this week's third divi is something in the region of seven hundred and fifty pounds.

That sort of money would be very welcome just after Christmas, Reggie thinks. With overtime, he earns just over a thousand pounds a year, so seven hundred and fifty would represent a tidy sum.

The team works diligently throughout the rest of the morning. By lunch, they've tracked down four winners, and by mid-afternoon this has risen to twelve. At 3.45p.m., when they've finally gone through every box, they report that they've tracked down fourteen lucky punters, who will split more than ten thousand pounds in prize money. This is the part of the job that gives Reggie the most satisfaction but sadly, his involvement ends with the delivery of the winning coupons to the verification team.

Handing over the winners to Veri is an important job, and nine times out of ten, Mr Hurworth assigns Reggie the responsibility of completing this onerous, multi-stepped task. First, Hurworth fills out a ledger, listing the winning names, and then Reggie is accompanied to the lift, which he takes up to the second floor, to be met by a receiving officer from Veri. This is all done to protect the company against any potential acts of fraud. The receiving officer is usually Laura Biggs, and it's an open secret that Reggie has more than a soft spot for her. In fact, Reggie often has a very hard spot for Laura, which he sometimes has to do his best to conceal.

'You off to see your bit on the side, Reggie?' Fred teases, like he always does without fail, and Reggie blushes as red as a Liverpool shirt, like he always does without fail. 'Slip her one for me, eh, Reg,' he adds with a whisper, turning Reggie a shade of crimson so deep, he wonders if he'll ever recover from it.

At the second floor, Reggie becomes excited upon being met by Laura. She's small without being petite, curvy without being fat and sexy without being improper. She has hazel eyes, a head of raven hair and dimpled cheeks, which capture her perfect smile. She's nicely spoken, too, her voice being warm, friendly, almost more seductive than her looks. To Reggie, she's Southport on a hot summer's afternoon, Prenton Park after a 3–0 win, and the smell of freshly cut grass and the first chilled lager of June. She's all that is, and could ever possibly be, good about the things in his world.

'Happy New Year, Mr Kellison,' she greets him. 'Are they all for me?' She smiles as he hands over the pile.

At first, as always, he's unable to say anything and just nods before finally forcing himself to speak. 'How was your New Year, Laura?'

'Oh, nice and quiet. I spent it with my mum, dad and a crowd of relatives around at our place. Thank you for asking.'

She's always polite. Never overly familiar, just polite.

'Mr Hurworth is buying us all a drink after work, if you fancy joining us?' he says, deciding on a whim to chance his luck.

She looks up from the pile of papers she's checking. 'Reggie, behave,' she scolds him playfully. 'I'd love to join you, but I'm babysitting for my aunt tonight. Some other time, OK?'

Although he's disappointed by her refusal, he's encouraged by the lack of a flat-out rejection. 'You just tell me when,' he says.

She eyes him curiously. 'Well, it's Tuesday today, so how about Thursday? A quick drink in Liverpool after work?'

It's more than he ever dared hope for. 'Deal,' he says.

She smiles and then quickly reverts to a more professional demeanour. 'All looks to be in order here, Mr Kellison. Please thank Mr Hurworth and the team for their help,' she says and then whispers, 'See you Thursday, five-fifteen, at the bus stop for Pier Head?'

'Glad to be of assistance, Miss Biggs.'

They part ways, and she looks back over her shoulder as she walks down the corridor, flashing him a smile.

1963 has much to offer, he thinks.

Later, in the pub, he's quiet, pensive; he's not sure if he's doing the right thing, yet this only adds to the excitement.

'What's with you, Reggie?' Fred asks. 'You seem far away, in the land of the fairies.'

'He's always like this after he's seen *Laura*,' Jenny says, emphasising the name to make it sound harsh and dirty.

'Steady on now, Jenny,' Hurworth interjects. 'I think Reggie has a lot on his mind, don't you, Reg? Baby's due any day now.'

'And Tranmere have got Chelsea in the Cup on Saturday, haven't they, Reggie?' Fred adds. 'Mind you, they'll need a couple of teams of Eskimos to play in this weather.'

'Yes,' Reggie forces a smile, 'to all of that. Baby is due, Tranmere with a big Cup game and not a husky in sight.'

'Cheer up, Reggie,' says Fred, 'it could always be worse. You could be a jumped-up plastic Tory, like Lord Haw-Haw here…' He gestures towards Morris.

The conversation moves on and despite not believing in very much, Reggie makes a mental note to go to confession on his way home on Wednesday evening. He needs absolution, even if he's not entirely convinced that he's doing wrong. Still, he suspects, all things being equal, that they are in fact sins in every sense of the word. He cannot absolve himself from the dangerous temptation that Laura represents, even if, in his heart, he knows that anything more than flirtation and friendship is just a fantasy. Yet, unlike all of his other fantasies, this one *could* be realised. He knows that Hugh Gaitskell is unlikely to invite him to join the shadow cabinet. He realises that his lack of pace, poor first touch and absence of any footballing skill means he's unlikely ever to play for Tranmere Rovers. But he holds out hope that simply being in the right place at the right time means Laura Biggs may be an achievable target. It's this, the possibility of delivery of the promise, that scares him most.

He's full of doubt now. *Why did I ask her to have a drink with me?* he asks himself. *I'm responsible for six kids!* He has a family life to maintain, and while she's not quite young enough to be his daughter, she's not far off it. Yes, she's pretty, and yes, she makes his heart beat that little bit faster, but so do John Manning and Barry Dyson and Eric Morecambe, and he wouldn't throw everything away for them. Why is Laura Biggs so special? Why is he risking everything being returned to sender? In his mind, he knows, just as Sir Edmund Hillary knew when it came to scaling Mount Everest, that it's because she's there. *If men didn't occasionally risk all to scale great heights, men would not be men. Men would be mice.*

Before long, he's homeward bound: bus to the Pier Head, ferry to Woodside, with the wind biting off the Mersey, doing a great impersonation of the Baltic Sea; 70a bus to Woodchurch and then in through the front door to minced beef, mashed potatoes and cabbage. He looks at Cathy, the woman who has so far delivered him five children – three boys and two girls – and who can boil a potato such that any flavour is removed, and who believes that cabbage is a dish best served pulped. Cathy, whose very reason for existence is to churn out baby after baby. Cathy and Reggie, once in love, now in life; once full of hope, now full of debt.

Burdened by the knowledge that there are lands where the sun shines, and a belief that vegetables can be cooked without losing all texture, the thought persists: *There must be more to life than this.*

FEBRUARY 1963

He looks carefully at the barbed wire. *Maybe five feet high*, he reckons. He can see the snow-capped peaks on the horizon. *Is that Switzerland, or just another part of occupied Germany?* According to his map, it's Switzerland, and Switzerland represents freedom; the chance to get back into this war and kick the Nazis back to the Rhine and beyond. He must get to Switzerland!

He turns the throttle on the BMW motorbike, and although 350cc is hardly enough power to give him the lift he needs, he figures that if he gets the angle right, approaching obliquely at forty-five degrees, he may just nail the ascent. He can hear the approaching German soldiers shouting at him, '*Nein*, English pig, you vill not escape, *ja*? You are not Steve McQueen, eh?'

He ignores them. He's not Steve McQueen, no, but he *is* Reggie Kellison, and he's not going to spend the rest of the war locked up with the Jerrys. The bike lurches forwards, and as it sails through the air, he knows the angle is perfect. He can see Laura on the other side of the fence, in a red headscarf, waving to him from the Swiss side.

Suddenly, there's crying, but not from him or Laura. These are the screams of an infant. *What's going on?* He's aware of the air around him turning colder than the Alps, and beneath him now is a bed, not a BMW motorbike.

'Reggie, it's your turn to see to baby David,' Cathy says, nudging him.

Switzerland will have to wait. The war is won anyway, and he has his own battles to fight.

He picks up baby David, who gurgles in recognition of the butler arriving to get rid of the shitty nappy clinging to his arse, and reflects on recent events. At the end of January, he'd received a memo from Mr Roberts, thanking him for the 'diligent work' he'd put into developing his proposal, but then explaining that after 'careful consideration', it had been decided, 'it didn't quite fit the direction we want to take our customers in across the summer months.'

He still doesn't really know what to make of that turn of phrase. It seems clumsy, if not false, and while he could well imagine Roberts using exactly those words, he's less than satisfied with the explanation given. Even worse, it also means that him and his family are likely to be stuck on the Woodchurch for the foreseeable future. All those kids leaves no room to save for a mortgage deposit, and with no rich uncle to leave them a pot of money unexpectedly – or even the odd sixpence found down the back of the sofa – they're stuck where they are.

On the plus side, he's managed to have a couple of drinks with Laura. The first, back in January, had gone well. She was very friendly, respectful and quite sweet, but she was also mature. She actually said to him outright, 'I don't mess around, Reggie. If you're serious about spending time with me, you need to think it all through.' This spoke to potential, but also risk.

He knows that she isn't the sort of girl to have an affair, nor does he want her to be. She isn't just some cheap tart out for a good time, and he's impressed that she's been for a drink to get to know him better not once, but twice. However, her honesty also exposes his own conservatism, as he doesn't really know if he's prepared to jeopardise everything; not when there's Barry,

Lynn, Vaughan, Reg Jr, Kay and now little David to think about.

He's deeply troubled and increasingly convinced that Cathy must know something. In this respect, he's guilty of overestimating either his wife's powers of reason or, more likely, her interest in anything beyond being a mother. So what if Reggie sometimes goes for a drink with his mates after work! As far as she's concerned, this is his privilege. He rarely comes home drunk, and he's often in a better mood after returning from the pub than on the nights when he comes straight home from work. They have nothing to save for that they could ever hope to afford, so the price of his drinks with Fred and chums seems worth paying.

These thoughts are still churning around in Reggie's head a few days later. The bitterly cold winter is playing havoc with the transport system, so much so that on this Tuesday morning in question, all of the team, with the exception of the Corpse, are already at the office when he arrives. As he approaches their area of the room, he sees them gathered around Lord Haw-Haw's desk in animated discussion.

'Sorry, Mr Hurworth,' Reggie says, 'the 70A was like being on the Cresta Run in Switzerland this morning.'

Hurworth has a strained look on his face as he turns to reply.

'Erm, it's alright, Reggie. Look, I can only say that I'm sorry.'

'Sorry?' Reggie asks, perplexed. 'No, Mr H, it's me who needs to be sorry. I'm the late one.'

'He's talking about this,' Fred pipes up, thrusting a Littlewoods marketing leaflet into Reggie's hand.

The leaflet has a picture of a cricketer striking a ball to a boundary and underneath it reads the caption: Our New Cricket Pool – It Will Knock You for Six! Reggie scans through it, seeing that it's a word-for-word copy of his idea.

'They're thieving bastards!' Fred says, not mincing his words. 'Hurworth, can't you get that friggin' jumped-up grammar school boy Roberts down here to face the music?'

'Mr Hughes! Language, please,' Hurworth chastises him. 'I know you're upset, but there's no need for such strong words.'

'No need?' Fred is incredulous. 'What do you suggest we do, Mr Hurworth, eh? Shall we have a game of snakes and ladders until we calm down? Have a cup of tea, perhaps, so that we can reflect on all this? I don't think so, eh?'

Hurworth looks flustered; there's not much he can do. Then, surprisingly, Lord Haw-Haw chips in:

'Do you want me to go and get him, Mr Hurworth?'

Fred and Reggie exchange a puzzled look.

'No, Mr Morris, that wouldn't be appropriate,' Hurworth sighs. 'I'll go and speak to his secretary.'

After Hurworth leaves, Lord Haw-Haw approaches Reggie, who's now sitting shell-shocked at his desk.

'Reggie, I know we don't see eye to eye on most things, but this is totally out of order.'

'This is typical of the ruling classes,' says Fred. 'They treat everybody like collateral, and then steal from and exploit us.'

Morris pulls a face.

'Fred means no harm, Jeff, lad,' Reggie says quietly to Haw-Haw. 'Just leave him be.'

Jeff nods, stoically accepting Reggie's judgement. Time passes, and eventually the Corpse arrives and is brought up to speed on what's been happening.

'Bad that,' he concludes. 'They're thieves, the lot of them.'

This sets Fred off again, which isn't exactly hard to do, and he's effing and blinding away when Roberts walks in, followed by Hurworth.

'Hughes, control your mouth,' Roberts orders.

Instead of shutting Fred up, this just makes matters worse.

'Control my mouth?' he cries. 'You – you have the gall to tell me about control, when you've just stolen a perfectly good idea from a man with six kids to feed? Do you know what you can do, Roberts, eh?'

Fred squares up to Roberts, the senior manager, and the scene is on the verge of getting out of control.

'Calm down, Fred, please,' Hurworth pleads, stepping in between the two men.

'Well, let's hear an explanation, eh?' Fred says. 'Then I'll think about calming down.'

Roberts turns to Reggie. 'Mr Kellison, I know how this might look to you, but I can assure you that this is *not* your proposal.'

'Well, I'm sorry, Mr Roberts, but it looks dead similar,' Reggie replies, just about managing to control his emotions.

'I agree,' Roberts concedes, and on that basis we're prepared to offer you one hundred pounds in compensation. Our proposal is entirely different.'

This sets Fred off again.

'Tell 'im to shove it where the sun don't shine, Reggie,' he yells. 'They're thieving bastards.'

'Hughes!' Roberts snaps. 'This really is your final warning!'

'Or what?' Fred challenges. 'You gonna take a thousand guineas from me? Do you know what, Roberts, fuck off with your thieving ways and your poxy bloody job. There's plenty of other places to work out there. I'm going straight to the *Echo* about this.'

With that, Fred turns on his heels, marches across to his desk and begins gathering up his belongings.

'Mr Roberts, I'm leaving, too,' Morris adds. 'Nothing disgusts me more than seeing people abused and exploited. You've two vacancies to fill now.'

Fred punches the air. 'You see, Roberts, we're not all so desperate to work here,' he says. 'Oh, and just to remind you of company policy, the going rate is a thousand guineas, got that?'

'As you don't work here any more, I'd be grateful if you left the premises, Hughes,' Roberts says through gritted teeth. 'Or else I'll have to call security.'

'As I no longer work here, you're lucky I'm not knocking seven shades out of you, jumped-up no-mark that you are!' Fred retorts.

All eyes are on Reggie, but economics mean that there's little he can do. He can't afford the luxury of walking and is worried that Cathy would think him mad for not accepting a hundred pounds. It wouldn't pay for a deposit on a house, but it would be more money than they'd ever had before. He stands frozen in the centre of the office, confused and uncertain.

Fred walks over and holds out his hand for Reggie to shake.

'You're stuck between a rock and a hard place, Reg. No hard feelings, whatever you decide. I'm off to the *Echo*.'

Reggie looks to Roberts. 'I'm not really convinced by your explanation, Mr Roberts. After all, it was you who said you didn't think the cricket idea was taking customers in the direction the business wanted to go. I need to think things through. May I have the rest of the morning off, on full pay?' He doesn't know what possessed him to chance asking for full pay.

'Yes, of course, Mr Kellison,' Roberts says, 'but I must remind you that as you're still an employee of this company, you're not allowed to talk to the press. Do you understand?'

'Nothing to stop me and comrade Haw-Haw having a chat with them, though, is there, eh?' Fred asks, grinning broadly.

'Only the laws around slander and libel,' Roberts answers.

'Oh, and the fact that we place large amounts of advertising with them, and give generously to their Christmas charity appeal.'

'We'll take our chances,' Haw-Haw says flatly as the unlikeliest alliance since Stalin and Hitler turn and leave the room together.

Roberts addresses the remaining members of the team.

'Right then, perhaps we can all get back to work.' He looks to Reggie. 'Mr Kellison, could you come and see me at two o'clock, please? We can talk further then, after you've had the chance to gather your thoughts.' He strides off, and an awkward silence descends upon the office.

'Mr Hurworth, how are we going to cope today?' Jenny asks. 'We'll be three staff down for the morning, and who knows where we'll be by the afternoon.'

The daunting prospect of the rest of the working day gives Reggie the cover he needs to exit discreetly. Hurworth nods to him as he slips out through the door, and although the supervisor looks worried, he also seems sympathetic towards Reggie's plight. *It must be hard for Hurworth*, Reggie thinks. *A decent man caught up in an indecent episode.*

Once outside, he realises there's nowhere to go in the Edge Lane area, and also that he's not a man who has much of a clue what to do with unexpected free time. Time is not a commodity that he's used to utilising; it offers choice, and this is a luxury he isn't accustomed to. It's as if he's being asked to decide which champagne to order, when all he's ever tasted is bitter.

Eventually, he finds himself on a bus headed for Liverpool city centre, but he still isn't sure exactly what it is he's doing. *What can I do?* he asks himself. He isn't like Fred or Lord Haw-Haw; he can't run the risk of not finding a new job. Having six mouths to feed removes the option of spontaneity, and then there's Cathy. He knows he can't simply say, 'I've had enough!' without her deciding that a wallop over the head with a frying pan would knock some sense into him.

At Pier Head, he contemplates taking the ferry, popping home and talking things through with Cathy. If this were a film, that's what he'd do. They'd talk sense, agree that they weren't powerless and then go to see a fancy lawyer in Hamilton Square; someone who lived in Heswall, in a big, fancy house, with two smiling children. In the final reel, the story would end with them celebrating with their thousand guineas, but he knows that this isn't the movies. He'd go home, Cathy would think he was sick, and she'd try to use him as an extra pair of hands to change David's stinking nappies. She doesn't do talking, she does pregnancy and babies.

Going home is not an option, he decides. Instead, he pulls the collar of his coat up high and walks under the Dockers' Umbrella, up James Street and across St George's flags, into the financial heart of Liverpool. The *Echo*'s offices are nearby, although he's not sure where exactly. He thinks about Fred and Lord Haw-Haw telling their story. *Will they be listened to?* he wonders. *Is it even a story?* More worryingly, he considers the possibility that Roberts was right about the newspapers being in the pocket of the Moores family, the Littlewoods owners. *I could well imagine it.* The further he walks, the less clarity he has. He's only getting colder and more confused.

It's 11a.m. now, and he only has an hour and a half before he needs to catch the bus back. *Sod it*, he thinks, *I'll treat myself to a tea at Reece's*.

To Reggie, Reece's Cafe is a step into a world that isn't his own. It's silver service, and the female staff, some of whom are very pretty, wear starched white aprons against their black outfits. Every customer is *sir* or *madam*, and prices are double what you pay anywhere else. He hopes that a refined

20

atmosphere will sort his unrefined head out.

He enters from the street outside, and immediately he knows it was the right decision. *This must be the only place in Liverpool not playing Beatles records*, he comments to himself. Instead, there's something classical playing. He doesn't know what it is, but he has an aspiration one day to be able to walk into a place like this and instantly remark to a waitress, 'Ah, Beethoven's Piano Concerto in D major, how nice.' If he were sharper, he'd realise that most of the staff don't know the difference between Beethoven and Battenberg. Most of them are so servile that he could announce, 'This is Tommy Steele's 2nd Symphony,' and they'd simply nod politely.

He removes his coat and sits by the window, staring out at the street beyond. It isn't a day for dawdling; there's still snow on the ground and a biting north wind cutting through. There are few shoppers about, and as the waitress brings him a toasted teacake and a pot of Darjeeling, he spots someone he neither expected nor wanted to see, at a distance or otherwise. *Rodney!*

Rodney is Cathy's brother – Rodney is everything that Reggie isn't. He's single, even though he's in his mid-thirties, and is handsome in the way that Scousers can be. He has a mop of curly blond hair, blue eyes and is tall – towering, even – like a good centre half, and he's confident in everything he does. The only thing Reggie likes about Rodney is that he, too, supports Tranmere. Everything else about him makes Reggie nervous.

He considers moving to another table, away from the window, but it's too late, he's been spotted. Rodney gives him a smile and a big thumbs up, and then he pulls a face while pointing at his watch and mouthing, 'Work?' A few seconds later, he's standing next to Reggie at his table.

'Hello, Reggie, lad,' Rodney says. 'You on the skive?'

'No, nothing like that,' Reggie answers, adding a false laugh to cover up his nervousness.

A young waitress approaches and says to Rodney, 'Would sir like something?'

Rodney beams a smile at her, and Reggie is sure she'll faint.

'Well, love, if it's not too much trouble, could I have a pot of your best roasted coffee, please, with cream?'

'Yes, of course, sir,' the girl says, smiling brightly. 'Would you like anything else?'

'Just your sweetest smile,' Rodney replies, and then as she's about to turn away, he adds, 'Love, can you turn the Mozart down a bit, too. I hate classical. Bet you wish it was the Beatles, anyway.'

'Oh, definitely,' she giggles as she wanders off to do his bidding.

This is Rodney in a nutshell: smooth, quick, the life and soul of the party, and exactly the sort of person Reggie didn't need to be around. Without being asked, Rodney gestures towards his bag and says, *'Please Please Me,* by the Beatles.'

'Who's that for, then? Reggie asks.

'Me, you daft sod,' Rodney laughs.

This is another thing Reggie doesn't get about Rodney. *How come he's buying kids' music at his age?* he thinks. *Is he ever going to grow up?*

'Anyway,' Rodney begins to probe, 'why are you here?'

Reggie decides that honesty is definitely not the best policy with a blabbermouth like Rodney. Anything he says will eventually get back to Cathy, so a white lie is the best option.

'Oh, my boss asked me to pick up some papers from a solicitor,' he says, wondering where the tall tale came from. 'We've got a dispute about a non-payout that I'm helping with, you see.'

'Oh aye? So, you're on expenses, like?'

Reggie nods. 'God, yes, I'd never come in here normally.'

The waitress returns with a pot of coffee.

'He'll pay.' Rodney nods in Reggie's direction.

'What?' Reggie almost chokes on his tea.

'When you bring the bill, just add it to his, OK, love?' Rodney instructs the waitress.

Reggie is beside himself. This will cost the best part of two shillings now, which is money he could do without spending.

'Help yourself, eh, Rodney?' he says as the waitress departs again.

'You're too honest for you own good, Reggie. You've got to learn to fall under the tackle, to win the odd penalty, you know?' He taps the side of his nose as he says this.

Reggie *is* too honest. He glances at his watch, and despite having an hour left, he decides to cut his little jaunt short.

'Got to dash,' he says.

'Oh, me, too,' Rodney grins. 'Time and tide wait for nobody when you're not working and all that.'

Soon, they're both out in the biting wind that has come down from Siberia to have a nose around Liverpool. Rodney nods a goodbye and leaves Reggie feeling like he's been mugged, and it suddenly occurs to him that his morning off hasn't provided any insight into what he should do about Roberts' offer. He's no further ahead and knows that he doesn't have many options. A wiser man would go into a solicitor's office and seek an urgent appointment, but Reggie isn't wise, or at least not worldly. He feels defeated, lost to his own self-pity, and is unsure what he should do next.

On the bus back to Littlewoods, he has no idea what he's going to say to Roberts. He doesn't have the words to express that he feels his idea has been stolen, that he has enough evidence to do something about it, or that Littlewoods have been less than fair in the way they've treated him.

Worse still, he doesn't have a spine, and he lacks the strength of personality to negotiate something better. He's a man in need of representation, either in the form of a union rep or a legal professional. He's also a man who, if he said 'boo' to a goose, would be worried that the goose would run rings around him in the ensuing argument.

This lack of resolve, lack of experience and lack of knowledge is a toxic cocktail that means he'll almost always find himself at the bottom of the pile in life. Worse again, and probably the most crushing aspect of this whole equation, is the fact that he knows it.

Back in the office, he hangs his coat up, but before he can so much as sit down, Mr Hurworth is at his side.

'Mr Roberts' PA has been on the phone,' he explains. 'He wants to see you in twenty minutes.'

Reggie nods the nod of a man who's been told that he'll soon face a firing squad; that dawn will bring a blindfold and a final cigarette, but no moment of passion with a local lady of the night. This is the hand he's been dealt. This is his fate.

Hurworth leads him up the stairs to the small lobby outside Mr Roberts' door, where his PA, Mrs Smart, sits at a small desk. Reggie has heard about Mrs Smart, but has never actually seen her before. She nods to him as he enters.

'Take a seat, Mr Kellison,' she says, indicating a leather-upholstered sofa.

Reggie is immediately filled with doubt. Does he sit at the end or in the middle? If it's the end, is it the end nearest to Roberts' door, or the one farthest away? Before he has time to make this less than crucial decision, the door swings open.

'Ah, Reggie,' Roberts smiles and then looks to Hurworth. 'I'll take it from here,' he says, dismissing his underling and leaving Reggie feeling even more nervous as he enters the office.

The room is very tidy; nothing is out of place. There are brown folders, neatly arranged, with various headings on the front. The one nearest to Roberts has 'Cricket Pool' written on the front and Reggie's name underneath.

'So,' Roberts begins, his tone gentle, 'what have you decided?'

Reggie would like to say that he needs more time. Somewhere deep in his psyche, he knows that this would be the best course of action, but he doesn't know how to ask for more time from a man as senior as Roberts.

'If I'm honest,' he says, 'I'm not sure.'

'I see.' Roberts alters his tone slightly before he surprises Reggie by adding, 'From what I understand, you walked around Liverpool for a few hours and then met somebody in Reece's Cafe. Was that a journalist?'

Reggie is taken aback. *How did I not notice anyone following me?* he thinks.

'It was my brother-in-law,' he says finally. 'He's not a journalist, he's a layabout. He doesn't work.'

Roberts looks unimpressed.

'Not according to the people I've spoken to.' He shakes his head. 'Could you verify his name and address, so that we can send somebody around to interview him?'

Reggie is getting flustered, but he knows this isn't right. If they interview Rodney, it's likely – no, absolute certainty – that the story will get back to Cathy, which is the last thing he wants. Under such duress, he discovers that he does, in fact, have a backbone.

'Look, Mr Roberts, you told me not to speak to the press and I didn't. I bumped into my brother-in-law by chance. He's not a journalist. He was out buying Beatles records. He then mugged me for coffee in Reece's. You know, given the circumstances, I am tempted to go to the police.'

It's now Roberts' turn to look surprised.

'The police?' he asks. 'Why would you go to the police?'

Reggie pauses before answering, hoping to give the impression that he's keeping his cards close to his chest, when in truth he's clueless as to why he made this suggestion. Luckily, the silence has the effect of increasing the stakes, forcing Roberts to speak next.

'Listen, Mr Kellison, I know that you think we've "stolen" your idea, but that would be a civil matter, not a criminal one. I don't think you should involve the police.'

Reggie senses that he has an advantage.

'Well, I don't think they'll be too impressed that you had me followed. It sounds more like the tactics of the Soviet Union, doesn't it?'

Roberts begins to respond, but Reggie takes a risk and interrupts him.

'Mr Roberts, I think we should both sleep on this.' He quotes a term he's heard used in the movies. In the movies, sleeping on things is always seen as a good idea. 'Maybe we can meet tomorrow and then have a proper discussion about what should happen next.'

'Very well,' Roberts sighs, 'if that's what you want. I must warn you, though, that the rules still apply. No speaking to the press and no going to the police. Is this acceptable to you?'

Reggie nods.

'I have a solid day of meetings tomorrow, so, with your permission, I'd like to schedule our meeting back here at five o'clock. I'll ask Mrs Smart to put it in my diary. You can go back to your desk now. We'll talk more tomorrow.'

Reggie's inexperience means that he's not sure how to end the meeting. Does he stand up and shake hands, stand up and leave, or what? In the end, he reverts back to his default position of servility.

'Thank you, Mr Roberts,' he says and then quickly leaves.

Out in the corridor, he's trembling a little. Where did he find the resolve to ask to sleep on it? *Reggie Kellison, bossing Mr Roberts around*, he laughed to himself, *and him saying 'with your permission', too!* He's never been asked for his permission before. What a turn-up.

He returns to his desk, and although Hurworth greets him with a nod, he says nothing. Reggie wonders if Mrs Smart had called down and filled Hurworth in on what had been said, or if Roberts will tell him later himself.

The afternoon passes in a blur, and it would be fair to say that Reggie isn't 100 per cent focused on what he's doing. He's more concerned about Cathy, and how she'll react when he tells her that the thousand guineas is actually going to be much less.

By the time he gets home that evening, he's decided that he'll put the best gloss on the story that he can. He arrives back at around six and is hanging his coat up in the hall, when Cathy emerges from the kitchen with baby David on her hip.

'Mince alright for dinner, love?' she asks.

He sighs. The joys of Cath's cooking are limitless. Mince, mince and mince again; mince done in a thousand different ways, with vegetables crucified to a pulp and lumpy mashed potatoes. The term *cordon bleu* would never be heard in the Kellison household. For Cathy, food is simply sustenance; the stuff that gives her energy to support boundless numbers of children and produce unlimited supplies of beef. The cows they devour die in vain, in comparison to those that grace the tables of fancy restaurants in Liverpool or Chester.

'I've some good news,' Reggie announces, trying to sound as cheery as possible.

'Really?' says Cathy, clearly not that interested.

Reggie presses home his disadvantage anyway.

'I've been offered a hundred pounds for that pools idea I had.'

'One hundred pounds? I thought you said they were going to give you a thousand guineas?'

Reggie is taken aback. He didn't think that she listened to much he said, and the idea that she has, over all these years, been paying attention leaves him a little dumbfounded.

'Well,' he continues, 'they've taken the idea and added to it, so I don't quite get the full thousand guineas, but a hundred quid is worth having, isn't it?'

Cathy looks unimpressed.

'Won't buy us a house, though, will it?'

Reggie is amazed. Cathy has never ever shown much of an interest in money, and now she's becoming all Reginald Maudling. He wonders if, any minute now, she'll start talking about the gold standard, or how Britain's economic prospects would be better served in the Common Market.

'So, love, you'd say no to a hundred quid?' he asks.

'I didn't say that, did I?' she replies testily. 'I said that one hundred pounds is not a thousand guineas. I'd rather have a thousand guineas.'

'So, you *would* take a hundred quid?'

'Look, Reggie, we're not on *Double Your Money*, are we? Stop messing around. You promised me much more, and now what are you promising me?'

He doesn't have the nous to understand the subtlety of Cathy's comment. She's talking about the 'much more in life' she'd been promised at the wedding altar. It wasn't supposed to be just a continuous round of babies' vomit and boiled mince, but Reggie isn't very good at nuance.

At this point, it might be worth asking what Reggie *is* very good at. It wouldn't take a learned scholar to quickly come to conclusions about his deficiencies, but what of his strengths?

To the untrained eye, these are not immediately apparent, albeit a smart appearance could be something you noticed about him. He's hardly dapper, but he's well-turned-out. Yes, despite sloping shoulders and an expanding waistband, he does dress smartly, boasting a clean shirt each day and a selection of work trousers. This isn't his own doing, mind, since Cathy bought, washed, ironed and generally serviced his wardrobe.

What of his other strengths? Loyalty is certainly a strong contender. He isn't just loyal to people, but also to institutions and ideals. He's always voted Labour, only ever considered Tranmere Rovers as his football team and, despite his left-leaning politics, insisted on the *Daily Express* as his newspaper of choice. Equally, for him, Sunday isn't Sunday without a copy of *The Observer*. Cathy baulks at the expense, but his favourite pastime is to read the paper from cover to cover, while listening to *Worldwide Sunday Favourites* on the BBC light service.

A commitment to self-improvement might also be added to Reggie's list of positives. This is something he doesn't just want for himself, but for his family, too. Barry, his eldest son, will soon be off to university, and Reggie wants all of his kids to do the same. He believes that education is the key to success – a door that, for him, has been bolted firmly shut. He left school at fourteen to work as a delivery boy for a butcher, but he suspects – no, he's convinced – that his life could have been different if he'd been given the chances that kids are getting now. He even secretly harbours a desire to gain O levels and retrain as a teacher, though he knows that Cathy would never entertain such highfalutin fantasies. They have six mouths to feed, and changing track is not an option.

Which brings us to Reggie's final strength: acceptance. While there are moments when he's annoyed by life – by the patronising stance of people like Mr Roberts, the lack of money and constant struggle – he accepts that this is the hand fate has dealt him. Of course, his politics means that he wants things to be different, but that's for the future. Now is a time for stoicism, not revolution. He still has his fantasies, of Laura, of riches and of a life beyond Woodchurch, but these notions mostly occupy his dreams, not his waking hours.

Now at the table, he's finished eating, and Cathy is piling the plates next to the sink for him to wash, stack and dry dutifully before putting them away. All across the nation, the same ritual is performed every night by men whose soul vanished decades before, but who still pass through something called life. Before he tackles the plates and cutlery, he bounces baby David on his knee.

'Who's-going-to-bash-Mr-Roberts-on-the-nose?' he chants.

The little mite giggles as Reggie repeats the refrain, moving his knee in time with the words. Baby David is enraptured, lost in the pleasure of the game being played with his dad.

I should tell him now, Reggie thinks. *I should burn all of his illusions in early childhood.* David needs to know, but his dad needs to pretend. Mr Roberts need not fear that his face will become swollen, as Reggie has neither the ability nor the courage even to raise his voice in anger. If he's to defeat Roberts, he needs other weapons.

It's five o'clock the following evening, and Reggie has been brooding since arriving at work. He's summoned all of his energy, strengthened by an afternoon drinking more tea than a man could normally consume: Chinese courage in lieu of Dutch.

As he makes his way to Roberts' office, he runs through his arguments again. He's decided that he'll settle for half the sum: five hundred guineas. This would, at the very least, give them something towards buying a house. He's sure of his position, and he plans to use the phrase 'my advisors tell me', if only to intimidate Roberts. He's drawn a line in the sand, and it's as fixed as a line in the sand can be. After all, if the sand is on a beach, there's the tide to consider, and if it's in the desert, the wind could blow it away.

He enters Roberts' office like a general commanding an invading army. He's confident, he's assured, he's in control…

'This is your doing, isn't it?' Roberts barks as he hands Reggie a copy of that night's *Echo*.

There is a diary column, written under the pseudonym 'Scally'. It reads:

> If, like me, the Littlewoods cricket proposal has knocked you for six, spare a thought for their humble employees. Scally has it on good authority that the person responsible is a man in the pools team, who will get nothing from his labours. Nice to see that one of the city's richest employers is not averse to sticking the knife into its staff.

Reggie looks up at Roberts. He's as white as a sheet.

'I told you, I haven't been to the *Echo*,' he says. 'I haven't spoken to anyone about this.'

'I don't believe you. I think you take us all for fools,' Roberts says menacingly. 'I told you yesterday not to go to the press, but you chose to ignore that advice. So, you leave me with no option. We will not, in the circumstances, pay you a penny. You've betrayed our trust, and you've dragged the good name of this company down into the gutter.'

Reggie is visibly crestfallen, but Roberts continues his tirade.

'If I could, I'd sack you. However, our lawyers advise me that I can't do this, but we're certainly not paying you for the cricket pool. Now, get out!'

31

'But... but I didn't talk to the *Echo*,' Reggie stammers. 'I talked to nobody, and then I came in here—'

'Kellison, do you not understand what "get out" means?' Roberts cuts him off. 'You're lucky to have a job still, so quit while you're ahead, otherwise you'll be a bigger fool than you can afford to realise.'

Reluctantly, Reggie moves to leave. He feels like Henry Cooper, floored on the canvas by a lucky punch from Cassius Clay. He's also angry; not with Roberts or with himself, but with Fred. Fred, he reckons, has betrayed him.

He leaves Roberts' office without even acknowledging Mrs Smart on the way out, convinced now that Fred is the one who must be punished. He doesn't have a phone, and he doesn't even write many letters, but as he leaves Roberts' office, he's determined to track down Fred and Lord Haw-Haw. He's furious with them. They've interfered in this matter for their own glory, not in his interest.

He storms back into the office and collects his belongings.

'Everything alright, Reggie?' Hurworth asks.

Reggie just glares back at him, saying nothing.

Instead of catching the bus to Pier Head, he gets one headed in the direction of Walton, where Fred lives. Within twenty minutes, he's hammering on Fred's door until his wife, Dot, answers.

'Hello, Reggie,' she says with a smile, 'is our house burning down?'

'Where is he?' Reggie demands. 'Where is that interfering, no-mark husband of yours?'

Dot raises her eyebrows and calls into the house, 'Fred, Reggie Kellison's at the door. He's come to murder you.'

She doesn't seem to be taking the situation too seriously.

Fred appears behind Dot. Framed in the doorway, they look like two hippos that have got stuck in a terraced house by accident.

'Hello, Reggie, mate. What's this about murdering me?' Fred says with a chortle.

Reggie thrusts the *Echo* at him.

'This! Why did you go to the *Echo*, eh? Why? This isn't your battle, this is mine. I was negotiating a payout with Roberts, but now you and that bloody Lord Haw-Haw have put an end to that.'

He's pacing up and down outside the front door and notices a few neighbours peering out from behind their net curtains, curious as to what might be happening.

Fred holds up his hands asking for calm, but Reggie's having none of it.

'Come on, you big bag of turd. I'm going to knock your head off!'

Dot bursts out laughing.

'Eh, come off it, Reggie, you're a quarter of Fred's size. It'll be like Laurel and Hardy!'

She's giggling away, and this makes Reggie even angrier. He takes off his coat, rolls up his shirtsleeves and raises his fists like a boxer.

'Keep out of this, Dot,' he growls. 'It's between me and your stupid husband.'

Fred's outside now.

'Reggie, we didn't go to the *Echo*,' he says. 'Me and Jeff both agreed that it would be daft to do so. Honestly, mate. We didn't.'

Reggie's flummoxed; his anger replaced by confusion. His arms drop to his side as he suddenly feels more like Tommy Cooper than Henry Cooper. Dot steps out into the street and wraps her enormous arms around him.

'Come on, let's have a cup of tea and sort this out, eh?' she says.

She steers Reggie through the door, and Fred follows close

33

behind, chuckling at what's just unfolded.

'Come on, Cassius,' he says, offering their guest a seat at the table. 'My life flashed before me when you threatened to knock my block off. Close shave, that.'

Over steaming mugs of tea and home-made ginger cake, Reggie explains everything that's happened. By the end of the story, he feels embarrassed about how stupid he's been, slinging accusations at a good mate like Fred. He knows in his heart that Fred isn't the sort of person to betray a friend.

'If it's in the Scally column in the *Echo*, somebody has told them about it,' says Fred, thinking out loud.

He and Reggie sit nodding sagely until Dot interrupts their musings.

'I'm not sure which one of you is Sherlock and who's Dr Watson,' she says, 'but what do you reckon, lads?'

They both look at her blankly, as if they've been asked to explain the basic principles of nuclear physics in Welsh.

'You've got me there,' Reggie answers, staring at the floor as though the threadbare carpet might throw up a few clues.

She turns to Fred. 'Well, love? Have you any ideas, eh?' she asks.

Fred simply shrugs his shoulders. 'No, love,' he eventually responds, 'I've no idea.'

'God,' she says, 'you two really are clueless, aren't you? I mean, can't you see? It's obvious!'

'What?' the men ask in unison.

'OK,' says Dot, 'who stands to save a thousand guineas if this story appears in the papers?'

'No, love, it's not like that,' Fred replies. 'It's Reggie who stands to lose a thousand guineas.'

'Oh, Fred,' she exclaims, 'where's that money coming from, eh? Think, who would have had to pay Reggie the thousand guineas for his cricket-pool idea?'

'Littlewoods,' Reggie answers, 'but, I don't think...' he begins and then pauses as the penny suddenly drops. 'Are you saying that Roberts has got the *Echo* to run this story?'

Dot smiles. 'Well,' she says, clapping her hands, 'there I was thinking you were a halfwit, but you've just shown you might be a three-quarter!'

'Bloody hell,' Reggie mutters, 'you might be right.'

'Of course I am. They expected our Fred to leak the story, but he didn't go through with it, so they called in a favour at the *Echo*. It's quite obvious, if you think about it.'

'Bastard!' Fred says, smacking the table with a clenched fist.

'Oi,' Dot warns, fixing her husband with a cold stare, 'save that kind of language for the pub!'

Fred blushes and bows his head apologetically.

'How can we prove it?' asks Reggie.

Fred looks across at his former colleague, sadness apparent in his eyes.

'Reggie, I think Dot's right, but proving it? Well, you know how these toffs are.'

This is the truth that Reggie doesn't want to face, but he knows it nonetheless. Now, there's nowhere for him to go but home; to wait at the bus stop in Walton and then cross the Mersey back to Woodchurch, knowing that life will continue to be a thankless grind through the ice and snow. No new home or happy ending; just a sense that those with power have struck yet another blow against the powerless.

MAY 1963

When defeated soldiers return from war, it's often hard to understand their feelings. Perhaps all the effort made and suffering endured was worth it for the victors, but for the defeated there's nothing but a sense that what's been endured was a waste of time and effort, and an injury to personal pride. You're not a war hero but a failure. You're not greeted as a conquering army, with garlands and people cheering you on the streets. You're greeted by the faces of those who know that your best efforts weren't good enough. The sense of waste is underpinned by a sense of shame. You have failed.

For several months, Reggie has felt like this. He drags himself through the days in a state of total dejection. Nothing gives him joy. Watching Tranmere play, which normally lifts his spirits – win, lose or draw – does nothing for him. Seeing baby David develop into a chuckling ball of fun fills him with indifference. Even sex is off his personal agenda, which in turn means that Cath is getting more and more annoyed. As for Laura, he avoids her. He allows others to take on the onerous task of delivering winning coupons to Veri now. To see her was to risk her discovering his defeat.

For her part, Laura is confused. She likes Reggie, but she wonders what she's done wrong. Of course, she's heard rumours about a dispute within the company, involving somebody in Reggie's team, but she hasn't linked the two issues together. To her, Reggie is just being *off*, and she has no idea of his own inner turmoil. She thinks maybe Tranmere are having another bad season, but all of her enquiries, and occasional reading of the *Football Echo*, indicate that it's been another average season at Prenton Park. There'd been signs of them possibly flirting with relegation, but mid-table comfort seems to be how it's panning out.

For Laura, though, Reggie's gentle, mild-mannered flirting has stopped. He doesn't understand that she's vulnerable. She knows she's pretty, but men are rarely as nice to her as Reggie has been. The only explanation she has is that she's done something to offend him.

After a truly terrible couple of months, the apple blossom came, Tranmere steered themselves away from the base of the table, and the cold, bitter winter gave way to a not-so-bad spring. While the sap isn't exactly rising for Reggie, he's slowly beginning to awaken from his torpor, and so it is that he finds himself at the final home game of the season: Tranmere vs Stockport. He's flicking through his match day programme, standing on the popular side of the ground, when he feels a prod against his shoulder. He knows that prod. He even has a name for it. *The Prod of Rod*, he thinks with a sigh.

'Hello, Rodney,' he says without much enthusiasm.

'Hello, soft lad,' Rodney bellows, prompting a few people to glance in their direction and smile at his enthusiasm. 'What do you reckon today, then? Ten bob says four–nil to us.'

'Behave,' Reggie says, dismissing the idea of a wager. 'I haven't got tuppence to spare, never mind ten bob.'

'I'll lend it you.'

'If I lose, I owe you a pound, and if I win, I owe you nothing?'

'Exactly. Go on, they'll never win four–nil.'

Reggie shakes Rodney's hand. 'You're on.'

They chat for a while longer, passing the time before kick-off, with Rodney running through the Stockport team, giving a reasonably well-informed assessment of each player. He finally gets to their goalie.

'He let five in last week, you know. Against Barrow, too!'

Reggie's worried. 'He never! Did he?'

'Only having you on, Reggie,' Rodney laughs. 'He let three in, but y'know, Barrow are useless.'

The game kicks off, and Rodney spends the whole of the first half yelling abuse at the players, the referee and linesman. Every time Stockport get a throw-in he yells, 'Foul throw!'

Eventually, Reggie has had enough.

'Rodney, have you ever read the rules of football, y'know, even a bit, like?'

Without a shade of embarrassment or a hint of irony, Rodney replies, 'Nah, I just like shouting stuff. Gets it out of your system, doesn't it.'

At half-time, Rodney wanders off and comes back with two cups of tea and a biscuit that only ever seems to be sold at Prenton Park: a Wagon Wheel.

'There you go, Reggie,' he says, still bubbling over with enthusiasm.

Reggie can't help feeling that, for the first time in ages, he's actually enjoying himself. It's a combination of Rodney's daftness and his unbridled enthusiasm for life. It's infectious.

The second half kicks off, and within five minutes Rovers are two–nil up. Ten minutes later, they get a penalty to make it three–nil. Reggie's beginning to feel a bit tense.

'One more goal and you owe me ten bob,' Rodney declares as the Stockport keeper retrieves the ball from the back of the net.

Reggie gives Rodney a weak half-smile and wonders how he'll explain to Cathy that he went to a football match and came back in debt. There's half an hour to go, and it's all Tranmere. With fifteen minutes left, Bell lofts a long ball forwards, and before Reggie can work out what's happened, the ball is in the back of the net. Just as the crowd go wild, he notices that the linesman has his flag up.

'Offside!' Reggie shouts, more in relief than anything else.

People around them give him a funny look, probably wondering why he's calling for an offside against his own team.

'Offside?' Rodney cries, but before Reggie can answer, the referee is walking across to the touchline, to talk to his assistant. They're in discussion for what seems like an age, until finally the referee points to the Stockport keeper and indicates a free kick. It's still three–nil.

'Cheating sod!' Rodney yells, but Reggie's pleased.

With five minutes left, the score is still three–nil. Rovers get a corner, which is only half cleared, and the ball bobbles around on the uneven surface before a County player lunges at it, only to send it ricocheting past his own goalkeeper. The ball is still mid-air when Reggie slumps down, realising that he has some explaining to do when he gets home. How could he lose so much money just watching a football match!

'You owe me ten bob,' Rodney shouts down his ear after snaking a long arm around his neck and pulling him into a celebratory embrace.

Reggie grimaces. It's all too much.

The remaining few minutes creep along, and Tranmere have now given up attacking. *Who can blame them?* Reggie thinks. Four goals represents a good afternoon's work. Then, in the dying seconds, the County centre half hoofs the ball forwards, more out of frustration than with any real sense of purpose, and when his opposite number in the Tranmere team attempts to bring it under control, he only manages to scuff it. The ball deflects backwards off the defender's boot, and the

Rovers goalkeeper, who's rooted to the spot, can only watch as the ball flies past him into the back of the net.

'Yes! Yes! Yes!' Reggie cheers, punching the air in joy.

All around him, the Rovers fans glare in disbelief. *Who is this madman?* they must be wondering. He was the only one not celebrating when the score went to four–nil, and now he's going wild at his own team conceding a goal.

A little boy, no older than six, walks up to Reggie and tugs at his coat.

Reggie looks down.

'You're mad you, mister,' the boy says.

And now everybody's laughing. Some of them even applaud what the kid has said, but Reggie doesn't care.

Rodney ruffles the boy's hair. 'You're dead right, son,' he says with a smile.

The final whistle goes, and Reggie is happy. Rodney fishes into his pocket and hands him a ten-shilling note.

'There you go, Reggie,' he says cheerfully, 'you'll have to buy us a pint now.'

After the game, they sip their pints in the Halfway House. Well, Reggie sips while Rodney gulps his beer down like a man who's come close to dying of thirst. Reggie ends up buying him another.

'So, Rockefeller, what are you going to spend your ten bob on?' Rodney enquires, grinning. 'A house in the Bahamas? A flat in Mayfair? Dinner at the Adelphi?'

'Oh, all those things, Rodney,' Reggie answers, 'not to mention a seat on the board at Rovers. Mind you, if you keep putting the beer down your neck like that, I won't even have my bus fare home.'

Rodney chuckles. 'Oh aye, mustn't squander your hard-earned winnings.' He raises his glass. 'Here's to the riches of the future and that poverty becomes a memory of the past.'

Reggie is taken aback by Rodney's fluency. This isn't the Rodney he knows. The Rodney he knows is far too flash for this kind of stuff.

'Do you ever wonder, doing the job you do, like,' Rodney says, 'do you ever wonder what it must feel like to win first divi?'

Reggie sighs. He's often wondered about it.

'If I won, the bastards would only take it off me anyway,' he answers, surprised by the venom in his voice.

Rodney looks shocked and gives him a quizzical look.

'Look, Rodney, you don't really need to know,' he says, having regained his composure. 'Anyway, as employees we're not allowed to enter. Risk of fraud and all that.'

'What, you mean you'd all go around the country banging in last-minute equalisers at games, to fit your entry?' Rodney chuckles to himself.

'No, not that way. There are other ways of fiddling the pools. I'm just not allowed to tell you what they are.'

Rodney tries to probe for details, but Reggie's having none of it. Rodney changes tack.

'So, if you're not allowed to enter, am I?'

'Yeah, of course. It only applies to immediate family, not to in-laws.'

'That's OK, then. I mean, if I won, I'd always make sure you and Cathy were sorted.' Rodney lets the comment hang in the air before continuing. 'First divi, though, I'd buy a nice house in Heswall, a decent motor and take myself off on a world cruise. That would just be for starters.'

'Yeah, Heswall would be nice,' Reggie agrees, getting swept up in the fantasy. 'Caldy would be even better, mind.'

'No decent pubs in Caldy, though,' Rodney counters. 'Heswall's got better pubs.'

'Is beer all you think about?'

41

'No, Reggie,' he says, looking serious, 'there's sex and football, too!'

They both smile and share a laugh – two men, fantasising about spending money they'll never have in places they'll never live. Then, Rodney surprises Reggie.

'I've been doing some reading recently, about the movement for civil rights for blacks in America. Anyway, there's this bloke called Martin Luther King, and he said in one of his speeches, "Some people have dreams and wake up. I have dreams and say, why not?" Good that, isn't it?'

Reggie's impressed. Not by the quote, which he's heard before, but by the fact that Rodney's reading about the American civil rights movement.

'Why you reading stuff like that, Rodney?'

'Music,' Rodney says. 'There's this bloke, Bob Dylan, singing stuff about America changing, and you need to know what's happening to know what he's singing about. Anyway, think about it. Heswall? Why not?' He glances at the clock on the wall. 'Bloody hell, I've got a date in the Cavern at half seven. Better get home and change, and get my backside over to Liverpool. Smashing afternoon, Reggie.' He stands quickly. 'Roll on next season.'

Reggie smiles. 'Good luck with the date.'

'Oh, I don't need much luck with this one,' Rodney says, adding a sly wink.

Then he's gone, out through the door onto Woodchurch Road, leaving Reggie to pull his jacket on and catch the bus back to Caldwell Drive, eight shillings up on the day. No house in Caldy or a flash motor, but tonight he'll treat his family to a fish and chips supper. *No need to wake*, he thinks, *no need to dream*.

Throughout the weekend, Reggie finds himself recalling the

conversation he'd had in the pub with Rodney. *Could this be a way of getting revenge on Littlewoods?* he wonders. He's only too aware about how to make a scam work, and he's run through the idea many times in his head, but he'd need a test run to see if it can be made to work. If he fails, he could risk going to prison, but if he succeeds, life opens up for him: property, holidays and money to set the kids up with the kind of life he never had. To him, money isn't the root of all evil but rather a means to stability and security. Isn't that what every parent wants for their kids? Is he wrong to use whatever means he can to get it?

*

By the time he returns to work on Monday morning, he has the basis of a plan hastily sketched out in his own mind, but not entirely thought through. He also knows that there's one other person who's vital to his chances of success. Consequently, when mid-afternoon comes and a volunteer is sought to take winning coupons through to Veri, his hand shoots up without hesitation.

'Well, Reggie, I think it would be a welcome return to the starting eleven if you were to deliver the coupons,' Hurworth says.

They exchange half-smiles as Reggie gathers up the small bundle of winning coupons and starts his mission. He takes the lift up to Veri, where Laura appears.

'Well, Mr Kellison, this *is* a pleasant surprise,' she says, smiling broadly. 'Where have you been hiding?'

Reggie is feeling bold, and he decides not to beat around the bush.

'I can only tell you about that away from here,' he says. 'A drink tomorrow night, after work?'

She moves in close and whispers into his ear, 'I'd like nothing better,' and then pulls away quickly. 'All in order there, Mr Kellison,' she says. 'I look forward to seeing you again *very* soon,' and with that she turns, and then looks back over her shoulder and mouths, 'Tomorrow.'

Reggie is at once both excited and guilty. This time, however, it's not the thought of betraying Cathy that haunts him. It's the intention of using Laura for his own means.

Reggie wakes early. He senses the warmth next to him, but he can't bring himself to touch and feel the soft, velvety skin that he so enjoyed the night before. He's still half asleep, and as he opens his eyes, he's greeted by the sight of his kids looking at him, mouths agape in horror at seeing their dad like this. He hates it when his subconscious does this to him. These waking dreams are cruel; they're mean, sad.

Yet, this isn't a dream. He's in the spare room of Laura's aunt's flat in Aigburth. Aunty Eileen is away in Llandudno, and Laura has borrowed the keys in order to sleep with Reggie for the first time. They haven't made love, but they've been intimate. They've explored each other's bodies, with Reggie delighting in the perfection of her youthfulness; of her pert bottom, small, firm breasts and flat stomach. Laura, for her part, didn't seem to be repulsed by the sagging body of an older man.

He expected to feel worse than he does; to feel guilty, remorseful, sad and much more, but he doesn't. He looks across at her, and he's neither sorry nor apologetic. He doesn't feel that he owes Cathy an apology. As far as she knows, he's at Fred's, having sought permission to have a fellas' night out and not have to worry about getting across the water to Woodchurch.

At the same time, given that Laura has only *slept* with him,

44

he doesn't feel he's used her. He feels more like a welcoming harbour for a ship in a storm. He's allowed her to explore an old place, and in return he's respected her, not abused her, and has resisted the temptation to plunder her treasures. She could still have a white wedding, even if the dress might be tinged with grey.

He moves his foot and in so doing wakes the princess from her slumber alongside him. She wakes with a smile, but then suddenly, realising Reggie's presence and that she's naked, she pulls the sheet up high under her chin, blushing scarlet in the process.

'I can't believe what we did,' she mumbles, shaking her head in disbelief.

Reggie strokes her hair; her gorgeous long, soft hair.

'It's OK,' he says gently, 'we didn't do anything too awful.'

'How can you say that?' she asks. 'I'll tell you something, Father O'Malley will have me saying Hail Marys for months for this. I daren't go to confession!'

'Bet you'll give him a secret thrill when you tell him about it all. I reckon most priests are perverts.'

She shoots him a slightly angry look. 'Reggie Kellison, the Holy Father Himself was once a priest. Are you saying that the Pope is a pervert? I'd ask that you don't mock my faith, particularly after what we've just done.'

He leans across and tries to kiss her on her forehead, but she pulls away.

'Oh no, none of that until you say sorry for calling the Holy Father a pervert,' she insists.

'I was only joking.'

'Well, I'm not.'

He mutters a half-arsed apology.

'No, that's not good enough. I want a proper apology. A clear one.'

He tries again and this time succeeds in placating her.

'You're meant to be a Catholic, too, aren't you?' she asks. 'You shouldn't be making nasty comments about our priests.'

Reggie isn't in the mood for a discussion about theology or faith. Neither is his strong point. He could explain to Laura that he never chose to be a Catholic; it was just the faith he was born into. He could also have explained that, to him, the Catholic identity is a heritage thing, and nothing to do with faith, but he has neither the want nor the need to get into all of that.

'I'm sorry,' he repeats.

They lie next to each other in silence, both gazing up at the ceiling in Aunty Eileen's spare room, and then Laura bursts out giggling.

'I think it does,' she says.

'What?' Reggie asks, confused. 'What does?'

'The ceiling. I think it does need decorating.'

She's in fits of laughter, and then she pulls the sheet away, straddles herself across Reggie and kisses him on the mouth.

'Come on,' she says, 'we need to get going. Look away while I put my nightie on.'

He falls into that confused space that men sometimes occupy. One moment she's straddling him naked, and the next she goes all modest on him. Hours earlier, she'd explored his body like no other woman ever had, and now she was almost as formal as when they were at work.

They finish an early morning tea in the kitchen, and it's still only seven thirty. They've agreed to leave separately, but, after some gentle persuasion from Reggie, they also promise that they'll do it again when the opportunity arises. *Mission accomplished*, he thinks.

As he makes his way to the bus stop, he reflects on his motivations. He needs to bring Laura in closer in order to

46

execute his plan, but the problem is that, at this moment in time, he isn't even sure what his plan is. All he knows is that it involves getting money out of Littlewoods in whatever way he can, and that this requires Laura and Rodney's compliance. Beyond that, he's still unsure how this will work. In truth, it's a less than half-baked idea, so much so that the ingredients are still in the cupboard waiting to be mixed. With that in mind, perhaps the best way to describe it is *embryonic*.

He starts to feel a bit guilty about what's happened between Laura and him. She's lovely, but he knows there are lines he can't cross with her. They won't ever have real sex, and he won't make promises that he'll leave Cathy and the kids for her. He's trying to be clear that he is, in some ways at least, a man of honour.

Meanwhile, as Laura is left cleaning up in Aunty Eileen's flat, she's clear in her intentions. She wants Reggie for herself, although she doesn't know why. He's not the most handsome of men, nor the brightest, if truth be told. He's sweet, though. She's impressed that he didn't plunder her treasures last night and that he held back.

That's the kind of man I want for a husband, she thinks, even though she knows he's far too old, and that if she were to marry him, she'd be excommunicated as a homewrecker, if not an out-and-out harlot. Yet, she wants him. Last night was simply her way of showing him how their life could be together, and, if necessary, she'll sacrifice even her most valuable asset to ensnare him. Nothing else matters.

Reggie considers the Woodside Hotel posh, but in truth it isn't. For Birkenhead it might be, but for most other towns, the Woodside Hotel would just about pass for average, bordering on a bit rough. It has a recently constructed glass lounge, which overlooks the Woodside Ferry landing stage to Liverpool and beyond. Not a bad view, but for the fact that steam from the trains at the neighbouring Woodside Station sometimes obscure it.

A train from Paddington has just arrived, and he can see the smoke billowing out from the station as he looks towards the ferry terminus. He's never been to London before. The farthest he's ever gone is down to Shrewsbury, once, to see Tranmere play. London remains a distant idea, a place where things happen that are reported on the radio but may as well be Timbuktu as far as he's concerned. He wants to go; he wants to see St Paul's Cathedral, Big Ben, the Royal Festival Hall, and all the other places he's heard about and dreamed about, but before that can happen, he needs his plan to work.

Just as he's about to drift off into more musings about his potential new life, he's interrupted by a booming voice from above.

'Do you have a valid ticket, sir?'

Reggie looks up and gets a shock, as standing before him, in one of the grandest uniforms imaginable, is none other than Fred.

'Flippin' 'eck, Fred,' he says, rising to offer his friend a firm handshake, 'you look smashing.'

'Makes a change from Littlewoods, doesn't it?' Fred chuckles, resplendent in his Mersey Ferries uniform, all gold braid and shining buttons.

Reggie can tell that Fred's brimming with pride and is made up to see that he's landed on his feet. A few minutes later, they're sitting with two beers, chatting away. Reggie realises how much he's missed Fred: Fred the joker, Fred the communist sympathiser, Fred the man who knows every swear word ever invented... Fred who would walk through walls for him.

'Fred, I need to ask you a favour,' he eventually says, after summoning up the courage.

'Reggie, for you, the answer's always going to be yes. So, what is it, chuck?'

'A couple of weeks ago – two weeks ago today, in fact – if Cathy ever asks, I stayed at your place, OK?'

Fred holds his hands up in protest. 'Hang on, Reggie, have you fallen in with the Krays? Why do you need an alibi?'

'I can't tell you. I just need you to cover for me.'

'No.'

'You just said that it was always going to be yes!'

'Yes, but I never said I was going to lie for you, did I? Lying for you isn't a favour. I can't do it unless I know why.'

'I can't tell you.'

'Well then, I'll just have to tell you to eff off, won't I?'

'Come on, Fred, it's nothing criminal.'

'What is it, then? Have you joined the Beatles? Were you out with Christine Keeler? Has James Bond invited you on a secret mission? Come on, Reggie, what have you friggin' been doing?'

'Let's just say that I was doing something that didn't involve Cathy but should have.'

'Are you not keeping your one-eyed snake under control, eh? So, you being married with six kids, you want me to lie for you? And what do I say to my missus, if and when we run into Cathy?'

'Hang on, our wives have never even met each other!'

'There's always a first time for everything.'

Their arguing gets more heated until a familiar voice breaks in between them.

'Eh up, soft lad, I thought that was your voice.'

It's Rodney, and without being asked, he's pulling up a chair to join them, much to Reggie's dismay.

'Hello Captain Pugwash,' Rodney says to Fred, glancing down at his uniform.

'Hi Rodney,' Reggie sighs, 'this is my mate, Fred. We used to work together at Littlewoods.'

'Oh yes,' says Rodney, 'isn't this the bloke you had your fellas night with a few weeks back? Well, thanks for the invite, eh?' he chuckles, not waiting for an answer.

'It wouldn't have been your scene, Rodney. Just a bunch of older blokes enjoying a few pints, eh, Fred?' Reggie says, giving Fred a pleading look.

Fred just nods, with no expression showing on his normally animated face.

'Oh well, let bygones be bygones,' Rodney says. 'Can I get you both a drink?'

'If you're offering, I'll have a pint of light ale, please,' Reggie smiles.

'What about you, Fred?' Rodney asks.

'No thanks, son, I'm not feeling right,' Fred says, looking directly at Reggie. 'Something just turned my stomach – left me feeling a bit sick.' He stands and nods to Reggie, and then shakes Rodney's hand. 'I'd better get back.'

Reggie reaches out to shake Fred's hand, but the gesture is ignored. Instead, Fred picks up his little haversack with a grimace and makes for the door.

'Sorry, Reggie,' Rodney shouts over from the bar, 'just realised that I've left me wallet at home. Can you get these?'

Reggie's too sad to challenge Rodney; too upset to ask him why he never seems to carry his weight when it's his turn to pay. Instead, he slaps a ten-bob note into his hand and follows after Fred.

'I'll just be a mo,' he tells his brother-in-law.

Next thing he knows, he's running towards the ferry terminus, shouting Fred's name. He's not fit, and the effort of chasing Fred leaves him breathless, but eventually he catches up.

'Fred, mate, come on.'

'Come on bloody what, Reggie?' Fred asks, red-faced and angry. 'Come on and be a lying bastard? Come on and help me be a gobshite? What exactly is it that you want me to do?'

'Fred, it's not what you think, I swear,' Reggie lies, knowing how desperately he needs Fred's cooperation – his complicity.

'And what do you think I fucking think, eh? Tell you what, if the tables were turned, if it were me asking you to do this, what would you say, eh? Would you say, "OK, Fred, that's what mates do?" Or would you be feeling like you'd stepped into the abyss, and that by telling one lie you know that you'll end up telling a million others, eh? Come on, give me an answer, Reggie, lad.'

'Have you never surprised your missus, Fred?' Reggie replies, experiencing a flash of inspiration. 'No, I don't suppose you have. You've never organised a surprise party for your eldest getting into university, have you?'

He looks Fred in the eye and can see that he's weighing it up.

'So, why didn't you tell me that in the first place?' Fred asks. 'Why the cloak-and-dagger crap?'

'I don't want to tempt fate. Y'know, nobody in our family has ever done A levels before, never mind gone to university. Call it daft, but I reckoned that if I told you, it would jinx our Barry's chances.'

'You daft ape,' Fred sighs heavily.

With that simple lie, Reggie has won Fred around. It's a lie that ignores the lust shared with Laura; a lie that sidesteps the deceit now concealed by a friend; a lie that means he'll have to spend ten pounds on a party to make sure he never got found out, but he knows that ten pounds is a price worth paying.

Rodney appears on the steps of the Woodside Hotel.

'Come on, Reggie,' he shouts, 'it's nearly time for another!'

Fred walks back towards the hotel with Reggie, and Reggie flings his arm around him. For a moment, they look like Morecambe and Wise walking on stage together. Reggie starts humming the *William Tell* overture, and for no reason other than the sheer daftness of it, Fred joins in. Before they know it, they're both running up the steps of the hotel, belting out *The Lone Ranger* theme tune in unison, while Rodney looks on, half amused and half bemused.

Poor Fred. You can be lied to by your kids, you can be lied to by your missus, and you can even be lied to by your parents. However, the most painful lies are the ones we tell ourselves. He doesn't want to think the worst of Reggie and end up severing their friendship, but there's a lingering doubt. He wonders, and he knows he has good reason.

Back in the bar, a pint is handed to Fred, which he raises to make a toast.

'To nights out with the lads, and secret plans.'

Rodney chinks glasses and starts gulping down his pint, failing to notice Reggie's embarrassed glance at Fred. Instead, he simply bangs his almost empty pint down onto the bar and eyes Fred hopefully, like a puppy hoping for a biscuit.

Rodney, Fred and Reggie, three men: one full of innocent hope and beer, one full of guilty suspicion and delusion, and one comfortable in his lies but full of intrigue.

Laura looks back at Reggie, incredulous at what she's just heard.

'You're going to do *what*?'

Luckily, they're not in a bedroom, and Reggie isn't suggesting a sexual act that may be illegal; although he's proposing something that could land them on the wrong side of the law. With that in mind, it's also fortunate that they're wandering around a quiet Sefton Park, with nobody to overhear their conversation.

'It's simple,' he says, 'but I'll need your help. Twice.'

'*Me*? What am I doing?' she asks, looking aghast. 'I can't even drive, so I can't be your getaway car. I can just about roller-skate, and to be honest, I'm not sure I'm cut out to be a gangster's moll.'

'There's no getaway car,' Reggie laughs. 'I just need you to slip something in, and if it works once, we can go for the big prize. A first divi.'

'Go on, then,' she says reluctantly, 'tell me your plan.'

Reggie explains that he's worked out a way whereby they can slip a coupon into the pile, which will be a first divi. He reckons he could slip this coupon in as a missed claim on a Monday, during their normal checks. The only problem is knowing when there's going to be eight score draws.

'And who gets the payment?' she asks, looking at him sceptically. 'I mean, it can't be you – that wouldn't be allowed. It can't be anyone working at the company, so who?'

'I'm working on that bit,' he tells her.

'And another thing…' she eyes him. 'What do I get out of it?'

Here, he does have an answer. 'Me,' he grins.

'Honestly?' she asks, after a moment's thought. 'You'd really leave your family for me?'

He doesn't truly know the answer to this. He only knows that he has to convince her that he would. He wants to explain that life's complicated, and although she's all he has dreamed of, he'd also never dream of not seeing his kids grow up and succeed.

'Laura, you know how I feel about you.'

This seems enough to placate her for the time being.

'Well,' she says eventually, 'seeing as though this plan is now really important, I think we need to start getting it a bit more solid. You're not exactly cut out to be a Great Train Robber, and I want to put my roller skates to good use.'

He smiles and leans across to give her a peck on her cheek, but she holds her hand up to block him.

'Not here, Reggie. Someone might see.'

She decides that if this is going to work, they have to be even more discreet and less public. They also need to find somebody willing to act as their deposit box; someone trustworthy, who can be relied upon.

'I thought maybe we could use Fred?' Reggie suggests.

'Red Fred, who you used to work with?' she laughs. 'Come on, Reggie, that's a bit too obvious, isn't it?'

He realises that she's probably right. Fred and he could easily be suspected of colluding. He needs somebody else.

Laura glances at her watch; it's 4p.m. and she needs to head back. Her Sunday afternoons at a friend's house, where her mum thinks she is, will be barred in future if she misses Mass.

'There's no rush. Be still before the Lord and wait patiently,' she says, a little too piously for his liking.

He's not even sure if she's talking about their plans for Littlewoods or their plans of being together. *Still*, he thinks, *no harm in playing along*.

'Amen to that,' he says.

'We might make a good Catholic out of you yet, Reggie Kellison,' she smiles broadly at him, but then refocuses her energy on getting home in time. 'Must go, otherwise my mum will have my guts for garters.'

She blows him a kiss and then heads off to confess a few, but not all, of her sins, and to give praise at Sunday Mass.

When Reggie needs peace and quiet, there are few places he can go. At home, the kids were always demanding attention, or there'd be Cath wanting some sort of help. At work, he was always too busy, and even his dreams, the perfect place for thinking, were filled up with passion for Laura. He had nowhere to go to really think things through properly.

Thinking isn't particularly popular among men of his generation. They just do things, rather than spend time thinking about them. Too much thinking could be seen as a recipe for vacillation. Too much pondering was a weakness, and yet if President Kennedy hadn't taken the time to think carefully twelve months earlier, the world could have come to a sticky, messy end. Thinking does have its advantages.

The only way Reggie can find time to think is by going out walking. He doesn't own a car, and doesn't care for drinking alone, so if he ever needs to think, he pulls an anorak on and heads off for some open space. He often wanders for miles, to Bidston Hill via the Mottely paths, to West Kirby by way of Frankby, or, if time is short, into the wilderness that is Arrowe Park.

Today, Reggie finds himself in Arrowe Park, standing near the big fishing lake, trying to work out who he can reel into his plan. One name keeps recurring time and again. This person isn't risk-free, but if he were caught, he'd have little to lose. Unlike Fred, or even Lord Haw-Haw, whom he'd previously considered, this man stands to lose nothing other than pride, possibly, but certainly not much else. The more he thinks about it, the more he realises that Rodney is the perfect accomplice. There's only one problem, though – one unmistakable, enormous problem – he's Cathy's brother.

He knows that Cath and Rodney aren't particularly close. They rarely see each other socially, and he's an occasional, rather than frequent, presence in their family life. In fact,

Rodney and Reggie see each other in and around Prenton Park more than they do at home; sometimes in the Halfway House after a match, and sometimes in the tea queue at half-time.

The three conspirators are sitting together in a pub on Seacombe Promenade, after Rodney suggested that they meet up to finalise their plans. It's the first time Laura has met Rodney and, ever the man about town, he's making her laugh, flattering her and generally turning on the charm. She responds with giggles, hand-over-the-mouth embarrassment and general good humour. For his part, Reggie is less than comfortable with this, if only because he's worried that his secret indiscretions with Laura will get back to Cathy. However, he also knows that Rodney and he keeping Laura sweet is a good insurance policy, as a way of maintaining her commitment to their scheme.

'Right, this is how I see the scheme working,' Reggie says, and he then goes on to explain the basic premise.

He'll smuggle a coupon, filled out in Rodney's name, into Littlewoods. It'll have to be completed on a Saturday evening, after the results have come out. They'll do a trial run to see if it works on a low dividend week, and if they get away with it, they can go for the big one: a first divi.

'Hmm,' Laura responds, not sounding too impressed, 'how will you get the coupon in?'

'Yes, that is a problem,' he agrees, knowing that security is exceptionally strict at Littlewoods.

Staff aren't allowed to bring in personal items unless they've been cleared by security, and this necessitates bag and haversack searches. They would easily find a forged coupon.

'Can't you put it in a personal letter that you need to post,' Rodney suggests, 'you know, like a birthday card?'

'They wouldn't let you do that,' Laura says, 'and you'd arouse suspicion if you went back to your locker before tea break.'

'Couldn't you smuggle it in in your bra?' Rodney asks, paying slightly too much attention to her chest.

'That wouldn't work, either.' She shook her head. 'It would have to have a stamp on it from Reggie's team before it came to me.'

They stare at the floor, looking like a local philosophy group on an afternoon out.

'What about your hearing aid?' Rodney says to Reggie.

Reggie tenses at the very mention of his hearing aid. He never uses the thing, even if it means that socially he's prone to missing more than the occasional word. A hearing aid for him is like a stigma, a sign that said he's unclean or unworthy of human contact. This is a totally irrational perspective but one that he maintains regardless. Like all irrational thoughts, there's no real evidence to support his belief, in much the same way that there's no evidence to support people's fear of spiders, mice or things that go bump in the night. Owning up to having mice in the house is akin to admitting to head lice, and most of us pull the bedclothes up higher when a floorboard creaks in the small hours. Fear is fear. It's irrational, yes, but it's something that can't be controlled, which is why it invariably plays a major role in people's downfalls.

Laura gives Reggie a quizzical look, which, if put into words, would have suggested a comment along the lines of, 'Not that this is a big deal, but why haven't you mentioned it?'

Reggie blushes. 'How d'you mean, Rodney?' he asks.

'Well, it's about the size of a ciggie packet, isn't it? Surely there'd be a way you could fit a coupon into it.'

'But then it wouldn't work. It would be useless,' Reggie says.

'Yeah,' Laura says gently, 'but not for our purpose. Think about it. Nobody would know it's not working, would they? And you can legitimately take it to your desk.'

Reggie mulls it over. It's a reasonable plan, aside from the fact that it involves him admitting to being deaf. He's uncertain if he wants to cross that threshold. After all, he gets by as things are. He misses the odd word here and there, but it's nothing to worry about, and he's comfortable with it. On the other hand, he's uncomfortable with his hearing aid. He feels it's the size of a coffin, not a cigarette packet. It reduces his social worth and kills his self-esteem.

'Mind, this one is bright, isn't she?' Rodney chips in, and Laura smiles a broad, satisfied smile.

Reggie agrees with Rodney's assessment. Laura's as sharp as one of Fanny Cradock's cookery knives.

'Let me sleep on it,' he says eventually.

Rodney stands. 'Another drink?' he suggests, beaming at their progress.

'Could I have a Babycham?' Laura asks, probably because she's seen the new advert on TV.

Reggie asks for a half of bitter, and Rodney sets off for the bar. He hasn't been gone for more than a few seconds before he returns.

'Reggie, I've left me wallet at home. Could you?'

It's almost like clockwork now. Reggie fishes into his pocket and pulls out a half-crown. Rodney looks at it as if he were hoping for a bit more.

'You'll have to have a half yourself,' he says, underlining his decision that he's no longer going to be a money tree for Rodney's bar tab. When it comes to buying drinks, Rodney's like a cheating centre forward, always playing for a penalty and never putting the ball in the back of the net. He's now alone with Laura.

'Why are you so worried about the hearing aid?' she asks. 'I mean, it makes no difference to me. I'll still think you're the same nice, kind, considerate and lovely man. What difference does it make if your ears don't work so well?'

Reggie smiles, but he doesn't have time to answer before Rodney's back with two pints and a Babycham.

'That took some doing,' Rodney laughs. 'Lucky that I know the barmaid, and she wouldn't let me have a half.' He bangs a threepenny bit down on the table. 'There you go, Rockefeller,' he grins. 'It's not what you know, it's who you know, eh?'

'He's a clever fella, your brother-in-law,' Laura says.

Now, the compliment has been returned and the bond is sealed. Mutual respect, and given the nature of the scheme being hatched, mutual trust. This spurs Reggie into a rearguard action, like a Rovers defender clearing the ball off the line and into touch.

'You know what, I'll use my hearing aid,' he declares, 'it's the perfect decoy.'

With this proclamation, he snatches victory from the jaws of defeat. Far from being the player the team carries, he's now George Yardley, the glamorous lynchpin upon whom the whole team relies.

Laura smiles over her glass. It's a smile straight from the movies. Reggie sees himself as the hero in his own film. Rodney was just a cheapskate with no style and no craft, who was always on the scrounge, like a sort of Harry H. Corbett. Reggie is more Cary Grant, without the height or good looks but with all the swagger and sophistication. Oddly, if you asked Rodney, he'd say he was the cool one, but his point of reference would be Albert Finney or, if he's over-egging the pudding, James Dean. To him, Reggie is Wilfred Brambell, AKA Steptoe, trying to pursue a pretty young woman who was way beyond his grasp.

JULY 1963

It is indeed around the size of a cigarette packet. It's small, worn on the body and, if arranged properly, almost discreet. However, the wire from the hearing aid to the earpiece is long, and about as subtle as a teenage girl at a Beatles concert, only instead of professing love and admiration, it screams, 'Different', 'Strange' and 'weirdo'. It whistles, too, all the time. Piercing and grating, and confined to the inside of Reggie's head.

When he first started wearing it to the office, some people changed towards him. It seemed as if they looked at him differently. No longer just the slightly dim office worker who sometimes wasn't very responsive, he was now the subject of charity, pity and, he imagined, probably derision.

'No wonder he seemed slow,' they'd say. 'He couldn't hear, could he?'

'You never mentioned this before,' Hurworth had said sympathetically.

'I've been struggling with it lately, Mr H,' Reggie had explained. 'When Fred was here, he used to cover for me – make sure I got the gist of stuff, but now that he's gone, it's harder to keep up.'

This was sort of true. Fred had always looked out for Reggie. He seemed to sense that he missed stuff and would often repeat what had been said for his friend's benefit. He was clever about it, though. For example, he'd say:

'What do you reckon to that, Reggie? Hurworth saying it's a first divi week.'

This brought Reggie in without being obvious. Some thought it was just the way he spoke, yet Reggie noticed he didn't do it with other people. He was grateful for that.

To begin with, Mr Hurworth was a bit patronising. He seemed to over-enunciate words and talk more slowly than usual, but only to Reggie. Yet it passed, and by the end of the first week things had returned to an even keel, and a few weeks after that, people had already forgotten. Reggie hasn't forgotten, though. He still sees the hearing aid as a stigma, like a sign declaring his reduced status. For everyone else, it's merely the source of an annoying, incessant whistling sound.

He discusses his feelings with Laura, while they're out on one of their occasional wanders together.

'I don't like being different,' he tells her by way of explanation. 'I don't like standing out and being seen as weird or anything like that.' He lets out a long sigh.

Laura smiles at him. 'Reggie, you're different,' she says. 'Most men I know are crude. They tell rude jokes or drink too much ale. They don't hold doors open for ladies, and they don't look well-turned-out. You're different in a very, very good way.'

It's now Reggie's turn to smile. 'Honestly?' he asks.

Laura answers by kissing him full on the lips.

'My kiss is the most honest response I can give you, and I don't care who sees me this time.'

Reggie feels emotional. He can sense the tears welling in his eyes. That someone could see him in such a way, well, he just finds it breathtaking – a thing of immense beauty.

Eventually, he gets his emotions in check and replies, 'You're a piece of heaven, you are,' and smiles.

Laura smiles back and, knowing that this is about as poetic as Reggie can be, kisses him again and then laughs.

'Now, don't go getting the wrong idea, Reggie Kellison,' she says. 'It's not all snogging with us angels, you know.'

They both laugh, but now they're back at the park gates. It's time for him to go back to Cathy and the kids, and for her to head home and dream of perfect futures.

As they approach the boundary of their secret life together, he remembers to tell her something else that's on his mind.

'I think it's time for us to do a dry run,' he says.

'"A dry run"?' she replies.

Even though she knows what he means, the shock of the proposition makes her repeat the comment.

'The Aussie pools have started now. They never have huge payouts, and it'll give us a chance to see if it all hangs together.'

'What if we get caught?'

'I'll take full responsibility, don't worry.'

She nods slowly, almost as if he's just told her that he'll go down in a hail of bullets for her. She places a hand on his shoulder and looks him straight in the eye.

'You're a good man, Reggie,' she says, but before he can respond, she spots her bus coming. 'Got to dash,' she smiles and runs off towards the bus stop.

We're not really cut out to be hardened criminals, he thinks. If they were, he'd have pulled her in close, his arm around her waist, and then kissed her passionately before holding her face and saying, 'Don't you ever forget, I'm not just a good man but the best man. The best you or any dame is gonna find in this one-eyed, no-hope city.'

Instead, he just waves after her.

'See you at work tomorrow,' he calls, but his voice is weak, blown by the wind into the polluted waters of the Mersey.

A few days later, on a warm July evening, Reggie, Rodney and Laura meet in a pub in Oxton, the Shrewsbury Arms, to plan their next steps. They sit out in the beer garden. Laura speaks first.

'I've been thinking. Rodney, do you actually do the pools?'

'No, love,' Rodney answers. 'They're fixed, in my opinion.'

Reggie and Laura exchange a glance and then burst out laughing.

'Are you taking the proverbial, Rodney?' Reggie asks.

'No, no. I've always believed it, and all this stuff confirms it.'

'Well, listen, then, Einstein,' Laura says to him, still grinning in disbelief. 'Can you start doing a coupon? Just a shilling a week. That's all you need to spend.'

'Alright, but you'll both have to contribute, or else I want a bigger share of the winnings.'

'Are you stupid, Rodney, or just ignorant?' Reggie asks.

'Don't get narky with me, Reggie,' Rodney retorts. 'It may not be much to you, but those shillings will add up to a few quid over time. I'm not working, remember, so where do you think the money's coming from?'

'You're not working because you're a lazy arse,' Reggie says, banging his glass down on the table.

'Shush,' Laura interjects, demanding the scowling men's attention. 'Let's think this through. We'll all pay ten bob into a kitty. That should keep us going up until Christmas, and then we can see where we are. Agreed?'

'Ten bob?' Rodney exclaims in horror, but Reggie cuts him off before he can say anything else.

'I'm in, and Laura must be as well, since she proposed it. You're outvoted, Rodney, so cough up.'

'The point is,' Laura explains to Rodney, 'if you don't do the pools, it'll arouse suspicion when your first entry wins, even if it is the Aussie one.'

Reggie nods in agreement and adds, 'The way I see it, we

test the system. We enter a coupon that isn't first divi on a random week in the summer. If we're lucky, we might win a few thousand, and if not, maybe a few hundred. Either way, we at least get our thirty bob back quite quickly.'

Rodney takes a moment to consider.

'If that's the case,' he says, 'can one of you lend me the ten bob, and I'll pay you back out of my winnings?'

Laura looks incredulous, and Reggie's furious.

'The word *cheapskate* could have been invented for you, couldn't it?' he says, looking like he's going to hit Rodney. Instead, he reaches into his pocket and pulls out a pound note. 'Laura, I'm appointing you as treasurer. This is mine and Rodney's payment. And you,' he turns to Rodney, 'can go and get another round in.'

Rodney leaves for the bar, and for once he doesn't return to claim that he's forgotten his wallet.

'I can't believe that man,' Laura says, 'he's so slimy. Are you sure he can be trusted?'

Reggie's equally exasperated.

'We can trust him, but he might end up being murdered before all of this is done.'

They both sigh.

'And all that about the pools being fixed,' she laughs, shaking her head in disbelief.

Rodney comes back from the bar.

'Your ale, your Babycham and mine here,' he says, placing the three drinks down.

Just as he's taking his first sip, a man walks past their table and waves.

'There you go, folks,' the stranger calls over as he heads towards the street, 'and enjoy them. Any friend of Rodney's is a friend of mine!'

'So,' Laura says, 'you didn't actually buy these?'

'Look, you can't stop an old mate buying you a drink, can you?' Rodney protests.

'Fair enough,' she says after a moment's pause. 'Just that next time we're out, you're getting the first round in, OK?'

Reggie smiles. He likes Laura's no-nonsense approach, and he knows that Rodney's too weak to argue back. *Things will change*, he thinks, even though anybody within fifty paces knows that Rodney's not the changing kind.

In the weeks following their meeting at the Shrewsbury Arms, Reggie perfects the numerous folds he'll have to make to a coupon in order to smuggle it in his hearing aid and then slip it to Jenny, who stacks the winners into a pile. He also realises that there's another problem to consider. The customer's expected to retain a copy of their coupon for their own records, and to present as proof of entry, but eventually he devises a scheme whereby he can pass these to Rodney retrospectively.

As luck would have it, and totally unplanned and out of the blue, Rodney won fifteen pounds in his third week of entering. Buoyed by this success, Reggie decides to wait a fortnight and then put in a forged winning coupon.

With the trial run approaching, he becomes increasingly tense and bad-tempered, but the date is set for Saturday, 20 July, and there's no going back. At work, he struggles to concentrate, so much so that on Friday, 19 July, Hurworth takes him to one side for a chat.

'Is everything OK, Reggie?' Hurworth asks, enunciating each word slowly and deliberately.

'Yes, Mr Hurworth,' Reggie answers, 'just not getting much sleep at the moment. Little David is plagued with colic. I'm a bit tired, that's all.'

'I thought you'd have been used to that, with having five others,' Hurworth smiles.

Reggie always finds it hard to be annoyed with Hurworth, who's such a good-natured man.

'No,' he says, 'it's like Tranmere getting beat. You know it's going to happen, but it still doesn't cushion the blow.'

Hurworth laughs. 'Well, Reggie, you know that if there's anything I can do, I'm more than willing to help.'

Reggie's worried now. *Will this scheme eventually harm Hurworth?* he wonders. *If we're found out, he could also get into trouble.* He's always assumed that what they're planning is a victimless crime, and the thought of there being consequences for Hurworth left him feeling cold.

Criminals need to lack a conscience, and those who continue to harbour one face the greatest risk. Stealing, murdering, cheating and such require that morality be left rotting in a corner, like a bruised apple. Reggie knows this, but it doesn't make his choices any easier.

At home that night, he was more tense than ever, and he finds himself shouting at the kids, making Kay cry and arguing with Barry about nuclear disarmament. His usual affability is replaced by ill temper and a sleepless night follows, which leaves him feeling worse still the following morning.

In summer, Saturdays at work normally finish by two. The Australian football results are in by late morning, and the number of entries is much less than what they get for the English competition. The first stage of the plan involves amending the coupon with the prerequisite number of crosses and then slipping it back into the pile for checking on Monday. This weekend there are nine score draws, so while not a first divi, it's likely to be a reasonable payout.

Reggie has informed Hurworth that he has a stomach upset and a touch of diarrhoea, and asked if it was OK if he could have more than the single allotted toilet break during the morning.

'Of course, Reggie,' Hurworth had responded. 'If you're too poorly, I can let you go home if need be.'

'If it's all the same to you, Mr Hurworth, I'd rather stay here. It's good to have a lavatory nearby.'

'Well, at least your hearing aid isn't whistling so much today.'

This is correct, but only because Reggie has taken the batteries out and concealed the coupon in the empty compartment.

When the time is right, he goes to the loo and marks Rodney's coupon with twelve score draws, nine of which are correct. He puts the coupon in, and now all he has to do is wait until Monday, when he'll take the pile of winning coupons to Laura, with Rodney's entry among them. There have been a couple of hiccups, not least the inordinate amount of interest that Hurworth has taken in his feigned diarrhoea, and on the way back to his desk, coupon folded neatly into his hearing aid, he's sweating cobs. He looks like a man who's just stepped out of a sauna fully clothed, but luckily the diarrhoea excuse enables him to pass this off as something he must be coming down with.

'Myxomatosis?' Hurworth suggests.

Back at his desk, Reggie discreetly removes the concealed coupon. People are used to seeing him fiddle with his hearing aid, so there's nothing new or suspicious about it. He pops the batteries back in and slips the coupon into a pile of other 'strays' that have been misplaced in the post. They're sorted into county and then district piles, ready for checking. He makes sure that he's given the coupon a worn look by folding it a few times extra, to fit the idea that it had strayed.

He pops the batteries back into his hearing aid, which starts whistling again. At this point, Hurworth wanders over to his desk.

Did he see me place the coupon? Reggie thinks, stiffening.

'Reggie,' Hurworth begins and then pauses for what seems a very long time.

'What is it, Mr Hurworth?' Reggie asks anxiously.

Hurworth raises his hands. 'Calm down now, man,' he says firmly. 'I just think you should go home. You're clearly not well, and given the circumstances, I'll make sure that you're paid up until two o'clock, OK?'

Reggie breathes a sigh of relief. 'Thank you, Mr Hurworth,' he says.

'Hopefully, you'll be feeling better by Monday,' Hurworth smiles. 'Now, take five minutes to tidy away, give any unchecked work to someone else and then you can go.'

Reggie's leaving the office ten minutes later.

'Have a good weekend, Reggie,' Hurworth calls. 'Somebody will be quite happy today, as it looks like it'll be a telephone claims week.'

Reggie smiles. Telephone claims mean that winners are expected to call in on Monday to a special number. This is the second-highest level of payout. There are two other categories below: postal and no claims. However, the rules of football pools also mean that the onus is on the company to check for winning coupons, too. Rodney's coupon would be identified this way, the story being that he's so lackadaisical that he never bothers to check for himself.

As Reggie reaches his bus stop, he contemplates what sort of win it might be. Not massive, but maybe around a year's pay, tax-free. Split three ways, that would be a welcome windfall. He just has to hope that the second stage of the plan will be a success on Monday.

AUGUST 1963

A warm August Saturday, one week before the football season is due to begin, finds Reggie, Rodney and Laura meeting in the Magazine, a pub on the seafront at Egremont. Success seems to have come too easily, as the previous day Rodney had received a cheque for £1,432, plus nine shillings and sixpence. It was a tidy sum, equal to around six months' pay for Reggie. Rodney has the crazy idea of withdrawing the money in one job lot.

'I don't believe in banks,' he explains, gripping a holdall underneath the table.

'You're mad,' Laura says. 'You can't just wander around the streets carrying that much money.'

'Of course I can,' Rodney insists. 'Who knows I've got the money, eh, soft girl?'

Laura has a point, and Reggie simply hasn't accounted for Rodney's stupidity. Still, he isn't going to allow this to get in the way of his plan.

'I've been thinking,' he says, speaking quietly so that both Rodney and Laura have to lean in close to hear him. 'I've been following the Great Train Robbers' story, and one of the things I've learned is that if you go to Spain, the plod can't drag you back.'

'It's called extradition,' Rodney says proudly, prompting Laura to give him a curious look.

'There are times where he could pass for being intelligent,' she says to Reggie.

'I'm not stupid,' Rodney cries, but Laura simply glances down at the holdall and says nothing.

'Right,' Reggie continues, 'when we do the big one, we need to work on the assumption that we could get caught. Not straight away, but after they've handed our winnings over.'

Laura turns ashen.

'So, I think we should find out what it costs to set up a base or hideaway on the Costa del Sol,' Reggie suggests.

'Now you're talking.' Rodney rubs his hands together.

'Not so fast, Trigger,' Reggie says. 'I was thinking that Laura could do the research by taking a holiday with her aunt. That trip'll come out of our winnings, and then Laura can report back.'

'What, like a gangster's moll?' Laura says, smiling.

'How much will that bloody cost?' Rodney asks.

'I reckon about seventy guineas,' Reggie estimates, 'which we split three ways from the pot.'

Rodney sighs very loudly. 'So, I've now spent nearly thirty quid so that her and her aunty get a holiday?'

'It's an investment, Rodney,' Reggie explains. 'We need to plan our escape route and work out the logistics.'

'Can't see our Cathy being happy about this,' Rodney mutters.

There was an awkward silence, which Rodney took to mean that Reggie hadn't heard him, so he repeated the statement.

'Cathy will do what she's told,' Reggie says quickly, 'but for the moment, I don't want her to know what's going on, do you understand?'

'Flippin' 'eck,' Rodney laughs, 'our Cath normally has to be persuaded to leave the house. Good luck getting her on a flight to Spain!'

Keen to change the subject, Laura interjects. 'We've got

something a bit more important to address,' she says. 'How are we going to split the cash? We can't do it here, so where are we going to do it?'

'Let's find a bench in the park,' Rodney suggests.

It isn't the most secure of places, but they finish their drinks and head off into warm sunshine in Vale Park.

To his credit, Rodney has already split the money into three equal bundles of mostly ten-pound notes, but with some five-pound and twenty-pound ones thrown in, too. Reggie's share is more money than he's ever held in his hand before, and luckily he has his work haversack with him. Laura's carrying a rather large handbag, and she manages to fit all of her share into it. Reggie and Rodney then each gave her thirty pounds to cover the cost of the reconnaissance mission to Spain. All the while, there are furtive glances to make sure that nobody's watching, but the park appears to be quiet. They agree that they'll meet again in a few weeks and prepare to go their separate ways.

'Don't go mad with your share,' Reggie says to Rodney, 'and please, not a word to Cathy.'

Rodney nods. 'Might buy myself a Ford Anglia,' he says, 'a new one. Or, I might get a second-hand Ford Zephyr.'

'I didn't know you could drive,' Laura says.

'Well, there's lots of things you don't know about me, Laura Biggs. Anyway, I can learn to drive, same as anyone else.'

'So, you can't drive?'

'I *can* drive, just not legally. Never taken me test.'

'Rodney, nothing shocks me about you any more,' Laura grins to herself.

'Right, I'm off.' Reggie stands and stretches. 'I'll walk you to the station, if you like, Laura?'

'I'm off to look at cars,' Rodney says. 'Should be able to drive you to the match next time, Reggie.'

Reggie smiles at that. A lift to Rovers would be much nicer than catching the bus.

'I won't hold my breath, Rodney,' he laughs.

On the walk to the station, Laura talks excitedly about Spain.

'I need to get a passport, buy some clothes and book my holiday,' she says. 'When do you think I should go?'

'I reckon September would be nice,' Reggie suggests. 'They get hot weather right up until the end of October.'

'Don't you want to come?' she asks.

Of course, he desperately wants to, but he knows it would arouse too much suspicion from Cath, and he doesn't think it wise to be away from work at the same time as Laura.

'No, you go with your aunt,' he says. 'There'll be plenty of time for us in the future.'

'You're such a sweet man, Reggie Kellison.'

Once Laura is safely on the train, Reggie decides to catch the number 18 bus back from New Brighton, and he wonders if he really is a sweet man. Here he is, contemplating leaving his wife and kids for a life elsewhere, which doesn't sound very sweet. What if he can't go through with it? What if, at the last moment, he realises that a life with Laura, effectively on the run, isn't what he's cut out for? Where would this leave Laura? Sweet men don't break girls' hearts, or at least not deliberately. As is his wont, instead of planning what to do with his money, he's now working out how to manage his guilt.

*

At this point, dear reader, we should turn our attention to Rodney. By now, you're probably getting the measure of him. He is, as we already know, a handsome man; women swoon for him, and he has an easy charm and a quick wit. He's a chancer, too, but as I say, you've likely worked all of this out on your own. I imagine you've also guessed that money burns a hole in his pocket, and alcohol loosens his tongue. These are not uncommon characteristics for men in the sixties, yet despite being occasionally clumsy, and sometimes given the appearance that the exact opposite is true, he's not stupid. He may be a nobody, but he's also nobody's fool.

This is 1964, and unlike in your modern world, jobs are plentiful and welfare benefits are relatively easy to acquire. In Liverpool, there's a black market within the job market, on building sites, roadworks and jobs around the docks. This is a city that's confident and brash, buoyed by the unparalleled fame of the Fab Four and basking in the success of its comedians. Askey, Tarbuck and Dodd, alongside John, Paul, George and Ringo, make Liverpool and Liverpudlians the kings of the universe.

Rodney, being a chancer, has taken advantage of all of this. He signs on, but also does the odd day's work here and there, driving trucks on building sites and painting houses as they're thrown up on the outskirts of the city. He charms women in the clubs and pubs of the city, often winning their favour, and he's not too bothered if they're married or not. Indeed, he rises to the challenge of married women, much as a mountaineer approaches the prospect of scaling new heights.

Rodney gets annoyed about things, too. His politics, while not radical, are very much communitarian. He hates prejudice and wants to see ordinary people do well, and he's dismissive of those who make a living by exploiting the weakest in society. He may be 'on the rob', but he only takes from those who can afford to carry the losses. Plus, he also gets annoyed by bad referees and condescending Evertonians or Liverpool supporters. He's Tranmere to the core, because, like his politics, he wants to support the little man, not those who already have an easy life with an easy path to success.

While Rodney's going to splash out a hundred quid on a car, he'll also stick to his budget. He's going to spend seventy-five pounds on a course in fitting central heating, as he reckons, quite rightly, that this is the way forward, because one day every house, old and new, will have it. He has no intention of fitting a system himself, but he needs the knowledge to make his investments work. As I told you, he really is nobody's fool.

Finally, Rodney's popular. He walks into a room, and people not only know him, but are also pleased to see him. They buy him drinks because they like this affable, funny and thoughtful man. He's never alone, and always gains respect, affection and friendship simply by being himself.

This is, however, 1964, when men can be men, but only in one way. If they try to be men in any other ways, they're ostracised and isolated. Rodney knows this, and while he's not unsuccessful with women, he'd like the opportunity not to have to be so guarded about his other *interests*. As this is 1964, you don't need me to spell it out. We know Rodney is living a lie, repressed by the conventions of his time. He's neither a 'fairy' nor a 'nancy boy', but simply a man of a certain persuasion living through the tyranny of his age. What worked for George Bernard Shaw or Christopher Isherwood, or even what worked for angry Joe Orton, cannot work for a Catholic, working-class guy in Liverpool. This is, as I keep reminding you, 1964.

Still, in his own happy-go-lucky way, Rodney isn't complaining. His life is good; unconventional, but good. He'll eventually buy not a Ford Zephyr, but a brand-new Mini, having fallen in love with the utilitarian nature and sheer pizazz of Issigoni's little car. He'll also be able to dress better and take even more care of his appearance as time goes on. He knows that soon his rim will overflow with the riches that

Reggie's scam will likely deliver. Life will change then, he's certain. Money buys freedom. This is 1964.

If you ask Rodney how he regards Reggie, you might be surprised by his response. He thinks Reggie's a good guy, a bit strait-laced, but good. His biggest question is how this good guy can stay married to Cathy, and he's been heard to say on more than one occasion, 'That Reggie deserves an OBE for being married to my sister.' However, if he knew about Reggie and Laura, he might still be annoyed. Rodney values loyalty, you see, even though he sort of knows that there's a special bond between Miss Biggs and Mr Kellison. Incidentally, he'd quite like a bond to develop between himself and Laura, but while he hasn't ruled out the possibility entirely, he does think it unlikely. Yet, dear reader, this is 1964, and you'll have to wait a bit longer to learn how this particular scenario pans out. Be patient.

For now, you've been told enough, possibly too much. More than Rodney would want you to know anyway, so please, keep his secrets to yourself, even when your tongue is loosened by alcohol. After all, this isn't 1964, isn't it?

SEPTEMBER 1964

Reggie has taken Barry to see Tranmere play, and as they make their way out of Prenton Park after another win in what's been a promising start to the season, they bump into Rodney.

'Hiya, Barry,' Rodney gushes. 'You're turning into a handsome fella, aren't you, eh?'

'Hello, Uncle Rodney,' Barry smiles bashfully, no doubt flattered by his uncle's kind words. 'Stuffy win, eh?'

'Nah, we were all over them,' Rodney insists. 'Useless ref, if you ask me.'

'I hear you have a car now, Rodney?' Reggie says.

They're walking up Woodchurch Lane, and just as Reggie asks the question, Rodney reaches into his pocket and fishes out a set of keys.

'And here it is,' he beams as they come to a stop in front of a white mini. 'Do you want a lift?'

'Have you passed your test yet?' Reggie asks.

Rodney glances around furtively. 'Sort of,' he says quietly.

'*Sort* of. What does that mean?'

'I'll pass it next week. I've borrowed a mate's licence for the time being.'

Reggie shakes his head in disbelief. 'I'll tell you what, Rodney. Pass your test first, and then we'll take a lift off you.'

Rodney looks momentarily crestfallen but regains his *joie de vivre* very quickly.

'So, how's teacher training at Exeter?' he asks Barry before adding, 'I'm actually studying, too, as it happens.'

Reggie waits for the punchline, but Barry gets there first.

'What, women's tits?'

Rodney laughs heartily. 'Oh, I'm always studying them. No, I've just started a course in central heating and plumbing over in Liverpool.'

'Good for you,' Barry says. 'Sounds like it's got prospects, yeah?'

Rodney chats on, seemingly pleased that his nephew is positive about his attempt at bettering himself.

'Anyway,' he concludes, 'you sure you don't want a lift back to Woody?'

'Next time, eh?' Reggie says. 'We're sticking around for a quick drink before heading home. He's off back to Exeter next week.'

They depart on good terms, with Rodney hopping into the car, crunching the gears and swerving out into traffic. He appears to have some way to go before he passes that test.

In the pub, Reggie and Barry enjoy one of those father-and-son moments over a pint. Reggie's extremely proud of Barry. Nobody else in the family has ever gone on to higher education, so that in itself is a great achievement.

'Uncle Rodney's going up in the world, isn't he?' Barry remarks.

'About time, too, don't you think?' Reggie laughs. 'He seems to have made a profession out of doing nothing,' he says before adding, 'Two more years and you'll be a teacher. I just hope I'm around to see it.'

'Wait, what? Are you ill?'

'No, no, I'm not ill. Just talking in general terms, you know.'

Barry doesn't know and becomes increasingly anxious.

'Look, I can handle information in confidence, Dad. It

won't get to Mum. Just tell me if something's wrong.'

'Honest to God, Barry, there's nothing wrong with me.'

'What *are* you on about, then?'

'Nowt, just talking daft.'

Barry looks unconvinced, but Reggie manages to steer the conversation back to football. They have a few more pints – more than they really should – and then decide to get fish and chips on Woodchurch Lane. They are, to put it mildly, somewhat pissed.

Staggering away from the chippy, food in hand, Reggie blurts out, 'I've put some money to one side for you. Not much, but—'

'Again?' Barry shouts, red-faced and upset. 'Why have you started this bullshit again?'

'I just want you to know...' Reggie begins but then gives up. 'Never mind, it's the ale talking.'

They stalk along Woodchurch Road, like two angry tigers munching on their prey.

'Sometimes, Dad, you're a right divvy,' Barry says through a mouthful of chips. 'You just say stuff, and it's like a bag of batter bits – mostly crap. Do you know what I mean?'

Reggie ponders this, searching for a clever rebuttal.

'I enjoy a bagful of batter,' is the best he can come up with.

PART 2

'It is only hope that is real, and reality is bitterness and a deceit'
William Makepeace Thackery

From: BJ Kellison
To: Tranmere-boy-down-under
Date: 23 January 2005

David,

I've found a few old letters recently. I'm not sure what to make of them.

Clearly, something is awry, and it might explain why Rodney's had no contact with Dad since 1965. There are letters between them that seem very angry and are full of cryptic references. Anyway, the last address we have for Rodney is in New Brighton, a suburb of Sydney.

I know that you're travelling, but give me a call. If need be, reverse the charges. Some of this stuff is too strange, and you need to know about it before you find one or both of them.

Barry.

PS: good win on Saturday!

From: Tranmere-boy-down-under
To: BJ Kellison
Date: 25 January 2005

Bazza,

I'm not wasting good beer money on phone calls. I'm popping into internet cafes most days to catch up on Rovers stuff. Just email me things.

I know you've mastered the art of switching a

computer on and off, and you've even got used to emailing. Might you consider investing/borrowing/robbing a device called a scanner? Dead easy to use, and it means that you can send me copies of some of these letters.

Let's face it, Rodney was a bit of a weird fella. We know nothing about his life in Oz, other than that he married. We also know he kept the faith with Rovers and until recently was posting as Rocky Ferry on the Rovers Rearguard forum. Last post he made was eighteen months back, in a thread about George Yardley.

I hung out in a sports bar in New Brighton the other day. They were showing Premier League matches and even had a live feed of a Liverpool game. I got talking to a couple of older blokes in there, and I asked them if they knew of any local Tranmere supporters. I kept it innocent, just making conversation. Oddly, they'd heard of Rovers, largely down to our cup exploits under Aldo. They'd even seen a couple of guys in the bar watching the Southampton cup game. They thought they might have been father and son. I have a hunch that one of them was Rodder, and the other was probably his kid.

Anyway, I'm going to ask in a few other places. Might even put my Rovers shirt on next time I'm in New Brighton.

Forgot to say, the women down here are amazing. Friendly and pretty, but impossible to shag.

Buy that scanner and let me have a look at these weird letters.

David

*

The view is why she'd bought the apartment. It looks straight out onto Darling Harbour, and she can see right along the quay, all the comings and goings. The place has changed a lot, but where hasn't?

When she'd first arrived in Sydney, back in 1965, the Opera House wasn't even built. It was a one-trick town, very exciting, very happening, and a place where you could really party seven days a week. There was alcohol, drugs, sex – everything. Back then, most of the people she met were expats looking to set down roots after getting cheap passage from England. *How that has changed*, she thinks. First it was the Greeks, and then the Indians, Vietnamese and Serbians, before finally more Brits again. The place is truly cosmopolitan, which is why she likes it.

Like her surroundings, she's changed, too. She's blonde now, not raven haired, though still managing to pass for a woman in her late fifties rather than her early seventies, and pleased to be doing so. She often wonders what would have happened to her had she stayed in Liverpool. *How would life have been?* She imagines that it would have consisted of babies, football and holidays in North Wales. She'd escaped it; escaped being trapped in a life that didn't fit, having found a trapdoor that led to the other side of the world.

Another thing she often thinks about is her final confession with Father O'Malley.

'Forgive me, Father, for I have sinned, and I'm about to commit an even bigger sin,' she'd told him.

Father O'Malley had no idea of the scale of the sin. He believed that at heart, Laura was a good, honest Catholic girl from an upstanding family.

'What sin is it that you are about to commit, child?' he'd asked.

'I can't tell you, Father, but it's heinous.'

'Does it involve sins of the flesh?' he'd asked with a bit too much interest for her liking.

'No, Father O'Brien, it does not. I just know that I will burn in Hell for what I am about to do.'

There'd been a long pause after that.

'Child,' the priest said gently, 'even if you have made a pact with the Devil Himself, you need to remember that the good Lord will always love you. He will forgive you your sins.'

'I know that God is forgiving and magnanimous. I just don't think I'll ever forgive myself for what I'm about to do.'

The rain was lashing down outside the church that day, just as it is in Darlinghurst today. Despite his best efforts, she was never able to tell Father O'Malley the details, and, in truth, she'd also never forgiven herself for what she'd done.

Yes, the intervening years had been kind. She'd enjoyed great luxuries and travelled to places she'd never imagined existed, yet she did so with the heaviest of hearts. Sometimes, the material rewards feel like adequate compensation for her guilt, but most of the time they don't.

Rodney is less weighed down by the guilt. In fact, once settled – which did take a while – his life in Sydney wasn't so different to the one he'd had back home. For the first few years he'd drifted around, living off their money, which never did seem to go down, and enjoying all that the new country had to offer. When he got bored of this, he started looking for a business to invest in, finally buying a couple of retail units down at the harbour, which eventually grew into a portfolio of properties. She never knew he had it in him to be so shrewd, but then he always was capable of surprising her.

They'd married, and their wedding was a solitary affair; just the two of them, and a business client acting as best man and witness. She was neither happy nor sad on this day – she just saw it as part of a process. They also changed their surname. First, she was Laura Yardley, and then it was Laura Beamish, until finally Laura Moore. She didn't realise it at the time, but he was choosing these names based on whoever the best Tranmere players were. They were his little private jokes, making cryptic references to their past. Their first house was called Steels Field, almost as if he were laying down clues, hoping to be found.

They stayed together for fifteen years; ten were happy and five weren't so great. At some point, they just stopped working as a pair. They were still friends – their dark secret meant that they'd always have a connection – but they realised that short of being partners in crime, and having a common link to their homeland, they were staying together for the sake of the money. Neither of them was malicious nor greedy, so when they split, the cash and assets were divided out between them on a sensible basis.

After that, she was left alone; wealthy but with few friends and no real sense of place or purpose. It took years of work, through Rotary clubs, business networks and the arts, to position herself among other Sydneysiders. Achieving this gave her a much-needed sense of pride, but despite taking a few lovers along the way, she never allowed anything to get too serious on that front. Her lingering guilt put paid to that.

She'd once been told that guilt is an unproductive emotion, and this is a truth that she can't avoid. There's nothing she can do with or about this feeling she has, just as there's nothing she can do to change her past. She accepts it, being a good Catholic girl and all, and carries it with her like a souvenir from her life in England.

What about you, reader? Have you ever felt a similar guilt, which has burdened and suffocated you? Well, multiply it by a hundred – no, a thousand, and then add more still, and I doubt you'll get close to how Laura feels about what she did to Reggie.

Ah, Reggie. The man who always scuffed the ball wide of life's open goals. The man left with his head in his hands, with only himself to blame. If the truth be told, it's a while before she's ready to talk about this. We have to be patient.

She often reflects on the last few days before it happened. Reggie had been oblivious. A brighter man, or perhaps a less trusting one, would have spotted the signs. Reggie, however, was almost childlike in the way he showed faith in others.

Nobody knew that the evening before was, in fact, the evening before. It was early October, and she and Reggie had met in a pub, the Basset Hound, which was one of his favourites. They arrived separately but sat together, gently touching thighs without holding hands. The conversation rattled on about how his eldest had just gone off to university in Exeter, and about his wife being tied up with their youngest. His life at home wasn't unhappy, but it wasn't what he wanted, either.

'I was looking in the wardrobe mirror yesterday,' he said. 'I wondered, if I could step into the mirror, would the world in there be the exact opposite of this? Then I got to thinking about what *this* is, and I realised that it was being married with too many children and not enough money, in a home that's too small, living a life that's totally dull in a marriage with no passion. The opposite would be you and me being together, alone, somewhere warm.'

'You'd miss your kids,' Laura laughed.

Reggie looked crestfallen for a moment.

'Sometimes I think you're mocking me,' he said with a hint of anger in his voice. 'Of course, I'll miss them. I love them. The idea that they'll hate me is like a red-hot poker being applied to my goolies, but the idea of life without you is even worse.'

Instead of arguing with him, and having judged the tone perfectly, she simply replied, 'You're dead soppy, you are,' and pecked him on the cheek.

Her final memory of Reggie was of him blushing and smiling, like a little boy who'd farted very loudly but was still adored by all the grown-ups in the room.

These days, while strolling through Darlinghurst and catching sight of herself in shop windows, she wonders how life could have been with Reggie by her side. Would she have grown bored with him? Would his wide-eyed excitement have become wearing? Maybe he'd have grown homesick for rainy days and Tranmere Rovers. The fact is, she doesn't know. He's her greatest regret, and that's all there is to it. Not some minor regret, like when you break a present from a maiden aunt, but a huge, gaping, mouth-as-wide-as-Sydney-Harbour regret, which some nights keeps you awake. Lesser women might confuse this sentiment with love, but she knows it's pure guilt.

That's not to say she never felt affection for Reggie, or that some of the physical things they did together didn't satisfy her. In the end, once he got over his own guilt, he wasn't a bad lover. He went about it slowly and carefully, but there were times when she just wanted to have her brains fucked out, and that wasn't Reggie. Every now and then, she wanted it a bit dark and dirty, and that certainly wasn't Reggie. She understands that, ultimately, once the money was in the bank, she would have grown bored of him, but also that her taking another lover would have destroyed him. She couldn't have done that.

Occasionally, on bright, sunny mornings, when she sits on her balcony drinking coffee and smoking a menthol cigarette, she can persuade herself that her actions were nothing more than an act of charity. The truth always catches up with her eventually, though. No amount of Hail Marys could make up for the pain she'd caused. The only recourse is to accept her guilt and wear it like a rosary.

Ignosce mihi, pater, quia peccavi absolve me, pater, quia peccavi. (Forgive me Father for I have sinned.)

MARCH 1964

'And finally, Kilmarnock three, Queen of the South three,' the announcer reads out.

Reggie gasps – *eight score draws*, he realises, *and no non-score draws. It's going to be a bumper week.* He feels his throat tighten, but there's no time for hesitation. He immediately asks Mr Hurworth if he can take a toilet break.

'I've been feeling queasy all day,' he explains.

'No problem, Reggie,' Hurworth nods. 'You do what you have to do.'

He can feel the sweat on the back of his neck bristling under the collar of his shirt as he slips the list of score draws into his pocket and makes his way to the toilet. He's practised this many times previously, and they've already been successful, so he knows it can be done. Yet, he still feels incredibly tense, to the point where he actually goes a bit faint and has to gasp for air once inside the cubicle. Somehow, though, he manages to put the two lines – they'd agreed on two lines – onto the coupon. The first has only five score draws, but the second has the magic eight.

He double-checks that the 'No Publicity' box is ticked and that Rodney's details have been entered correctly. This is never a foregone conclusion, since Rodney could barely enter a urinal without creating chaos. All of this is done within the space of three minutes, after which he folds the completed coupon, places it back into the hearing-aid box and returns to his desk.

'Better?' Hurworth asks as Reggie sits down.

'Aye,' Reggie says.

'I see your lot got beat again.'

'Nothing changes, Mr Hurworth,' Reggie grins, knowing now that *everything* is about to change.

After work, he heads straight home, and on the bus down to Pier Head he tries to figure out how long the whole process will take. The win would be confirmed by next week, and then the money will be with Rodney within three weeks. He reckons that everything will be sorted by the end of April. He'll need to start looking for another job soon, and Fred has already said that he can get him in at the Woodside terminal. It'll just be as a ticket inspector, but he doesn't mind. It'll only be for a couple of weeks, and he'll be falling 'sick' towards the end of the second week anyway.

He loves late March. The evenings are light, and there's a hint of spring in the air. As he crosses the river on the ferry, he wonders how long it'll be before he'll be alone with Laura, away from his family. *With Laura!* he thinks, allowing himself a sly grin. The grin is still present when he gets back to Caldwell Drive, right up until he puts his little haversack down in the hall and hears a familiar voice booming from the kitchen.

'Look what the cat dragged in,' Rodney proclaims from the head of the kitchen table, where he and Cathy are enjoying tea and jam butties. 'You alright, Reggie?'

'Great,' Reggie says flatly, not having expected to see Rodney today. 'Any chance of a cup of tea, Cathy?' he asks, pulling up a chair as the tea is poured.

'So, have you created any rich men today, Reggie?' Rodney asks.

'Eight score draws,' Reggie says, trying to be deadpan but struggling to hide the fact that he suspects Rodney knows it's a first-divi week.

'Go on?' Rodney blows the air out of his cheeks. 'I'll have to check me coupon when I get home, won't I?' he says and turns to address the kids. 'You could be looking at a very wealthy uncle here, you know.'

The kids giggle, and then little Kay speaks up.

'Uncle Rodney, Mum says you're always broke and you haven't got a pot to piss in.'

'*Kay*!' Cathy shrieks, but Rodney just laughs.

'Did she now?' he asks Kay with a massive grin on his face. 'She's not very nice, my sister, is she?' He tousles the little girl's hair and winks at his sister. 'I do have a pot, but I don't always have loo paper. But then that's what the *Daily Express* is for, isn't it?'

At this, everybody laughs, including Reggie. The tension is broken between Rodney and him, and, not for the first time, he wishes he was as quick-witted as his brother-in-law.

Rodney stays for another hour or so, and as he's leaving, he starts to talk to Reggie about Tranmere.

'You coming on Tuesday?' he asks. 'It's just that we can decide if we're going to any away games before the end of the season.'

'I don't think I can afford that, Rodney,' Reggie replies, not playing along.

Rodney grimaces. 'Well, just come along anyway, eh? I'll buy you a pint at the Halfway before the match and—'

'Every time you offer to buy me a drink, it ends up costing *me* money.' Reggie cuts him off. 'How does that work, eh?'

Rodney drops his voice to a whisper, which makes it hard for Reggie to hear, given his impairment.

'We need to talk about *stuff*,' he hisses, over-enunciating to the point that he looks like a demented goldfish.

Reggie shakes his head in disbelief and resolves to remain firm.

'Look, *Rockefeller*,' he says, coining one of Rodney's favourite phrases, 'just give it time. You'll be contacted soon enough, OK?'

At this point, Cathy enters the hallway.

'What will he be contacted about?'

'I'm thinking of buying me first season ticket next season,' Rodney says, thinking on his feet. 'You know, I was just asking Reggie how it works, like.'

Cathy gives Reggie a stern look.

'I hope you're not thinking of getting one, Reggie Kellison. Our Rodney might have got himself a pot, but you're doing it up the wall by comparison, if you get my drift?'

She smirks at her own clever remark, and Reggie's mind instantly flashes to an image of Laura's warm smile. He could almost hear her saying, 'Be calm. This doesn't matter.'

Taking Laura's advice, he nods his approval and laughs along.

'I'm just hoping that Rodney will lend me his when he gets bored of going,' he says. 'I know we can't afford it. As the song sort of says, "I'm not half the fan Rodney used to be."'

'Eh?' Cathy doesn't get it.

'Look at you, Reggie,' Rodney laughs, 'trying to quote the Beatles, eh? You'll be growing your hair long and going off to India soon.'

'"Help me get my teeth back on the ground," eh, Rodney?'

Rodney interrupted him. 'Reggie, there's no point, you're not hip and with your dodgy hearing you'll get everything wrong, soft lad!' he shouts, as Cathy shows him to the door.

'I prefer Cilla Black,' she says, but Reggie isn't listening.

He's thinking about Laura. *Laura's hair, Laura's breasts – Laura and him in the future, together.*

Rodney really does want to talk to Reggie. He's starting to feel guilty, and now that the deed is about to be done, he wants to try to set things straight, to soften the eventual blow. This isn't how it was supposed to go, but during one of their evenings down the pub, Rodney and Laura had got talking after Reggie had gone back to Woodchurch.

'I wouldn't have thought Reggie was your type,' he'd said offhandedly.

Laura took offence to this.

'I don't have a *type*,' she'd snapped. 'Your Reggie is kind, gentle and always treats me like a lady. That's my *type*. A man who knows how to respect me.'

Rodney was a bit taken aback by her ferocity.

'I didn't mean anything by it, like,' he said, holding his hands up in surrender.

'Maybe not, but you're too quick to judge. Anyway, what's your type, seeing as you think everyone else has one?'

He thought long and hard before answering.

'Can I be honest?' he asked, his voice dropping to barely a whisper.

'Of course,' she said, lowering her tone to match his.

'Well, let's just say it isn't you.'

'Why, what's wrong with me?'

Rodney again found himself apologising.

'Oh, there's nothing *wrong* with you, Laura. You're beautiful, you're funny – you're every man's dream, with your dark eyes and luscious hair.'

'Go on, then, what is it? Do you prefer blondes?'

'Not really, no. I—'

'Is it redheads? Is that what you like?'

He shook his head. 'Do you know the Beatles?' he asked.

'Of course I know the Beatles!'

'So, do you know their manager?'

'Brian Epstein?'

'That's right,' he nodded. 'Well, I go to the same sort of places he goes to.'

'Well, that doesn't tell me much, does it?'

'What do you know about Brian?'

'He dresses well, owns a record shop and is a bachelor, not much else. Oh, and of course he manages the Beatles and Cilla.'

Rodney sighed, long and deep.

'Come on,' she pressed, 'what else, then?'

Rodney took a gulp of his beer.

'He doesn't like women.'

Laura looked at him, her face a picture of confusion.

'But, if he doesn't like women, what...' There was the silent sound of a penny dropping as the look on Laura's face changed. 'You mean he...' She looked at Rodney in disbelief before clasping a hand over her mouth. 'Oh, my goodness,' she giggled and then went silent for a moment. 'What's this got to do with you, though?' she eventually asked.

Rodney squirmed. *Why is she making this so difficult?* he wonders.

'I'm the same way,' he said, barely audible now.

'What, you're—'

'Shush,' Rodney said, whipping his head around to make sure no one was listening.

'But, you're dead handsome and lovely and... seriously, you're a poof?'

She blew her cheeks out as she said this. She looked flabbergasted.

'I prefer *queer*,' he said.

That's where their first conversation began, with Rodney explaining to Laura the niceties of being gay at a time when homosexuality was still illegal. Laura had asked the usual questions: was he sure? When did he first know? Did his family know?

Rodney answered all of her questions as she asked them. It was nearly closing time by the time they'd finished.

'So, this *thing*,' she said, lowering her voice again. 'This pools thing is a big opportunity for you?'

'I suppose so, yes,' he said. 'It'll be more money than I've ever known. I could go abroad, somewhere where being myself wouldn't be such a problem.'

That night in the pub was when Laura knew.

She had, of course, always had her doubts. She really didn't want to be the woman to take a man from his wife and six kids; the thought of being a marriage wrecker was horrifying to her. It went against all of her values, and not just the Catholic ones. Obviously, her faith loomed large whenever she thought of the consequences of her actions, but so did her guilt as a woman. How could she live with leaving six kids with no dad and a wife with no husband? It just seemed wrong on so many levels, and now she had the opportunity to atone for her sins and instead rescue Rodney. She loved Reggie, but she believed that depriving six innocent children of a father was far worse than breaking a man's heart. It was something that had been keeping her awake at night, and would no doubt keep her awake for many nights into the future if she went through with it.

As time went by, she and Rodney hatched their own plan. The money was going to him anyway, so that was half the battle. All that was left was finding a way to cut Reggie out. For his part, Rodney felt no guilt. Cathy was his sister, and he couldn't stand by and let his nephews and nieces suffer while their dad abandoned them. The more they talked, the clearer it became that his best option was to leave Birkenhead behind and emerge from the shadows somewhere new, with Laura serving as the perfect foil. He could take her with him and quietly live the lie he craved.

*

Meanwhile, Reggie definitely isn't going to the game with Rodney on Tuesday night. *Why would he even suggest it?* he thinks. It would be stupid to be seen in public with the recipient of such a large win: *one hundred and fifty-two grand!* It's not as big a win as Viv Nicholson, but enough to live on for a lifetime. Soon, he and Laura will start their new life together, and he'll see her smiling face every day, kiss her soft lips every morning and feel her warmth beside him every night. The money is secondary to all of that.

Oh, Reggie. If only you'd been alert and awake to what was going on around you. Unfortunately, though, you were a dreamer, but you weren't the only one!

*

From: BJ Kellison
To: Tranmere-boy-down-under
Date: 30 January 2005

Just back from Currys with a scanner. You were right; they're not too expensive.

Not sure what progress you're making, but the correspondence gets more and more aggressive. Rodney seems to be very angry towards Dad, for some reason. If you do track him down, don't be surprised if he doesn't want to see you.

From what I can gather, he's married to a girl who's also from Liverpool. There's a pile of letters to read through, though.

This weekend's games were all postponed. Lucky for your lot, since they keep getting beat. Dad's slipping in and out of consciousness. Not sure if he's getting better or worse, but the doctors are 'optimistic'. Make of that what you will.

Barry

From: Tranmere-boy-down-under
To: BJ Kellison
Date: 1 February 2005

Bazza,

Currys? Who buys a scanner in Curry's?! You should have bought it online. You don't half know how to waste money.

Somebody I met in New Brighton thinks they know a woman who used to go out with a Tranmere supporter. It was years ago, and they've now split up. I might track her down, as you never know.

Sorry that Dad's still poorly. Doing my best to locate Rodders.

Look forward to getting those letters.

David

*

They have a well-conceived plan, albeit it's more like something out of *The Pink Panther* than *James Bond*. Nonetheless, there's a structure to how Reggie's share of the winnings will get from Rodney to him without raising suspicion. The first thing Reggie had to do was set up a bank account under a false name, and getting the documentation together for that had been relatively easy. At school, he'd had a classmate, Bobby Grant, who died of yellow fever, and so he opened an account using a copy of the deceased boy's birth certificate as proof of identity. This may seem odd now, but in 1964 there were very few ways of verifying a person's details. Once Reggie had the birth certificate, he was then able to get a false passport to match.

When the time's right, Rodney is to transfer two thirds of the winnings into the Grant account. There are rumours that the win is approximately a hundred and forty-eight thousand, which would earn Rodney around forty-nine thousand, although Reggie is of a mind to round the figure up to fifty thousand, just to keep things simple. He's now working at the Woodside ferry terminal as a ticket inspector, a job he'd been doing for a week. Fred was true to his word, and he'd walked into the job with very little hassle. Of course, Mr Hurworth had been extremely disappointed to learn that Reggie was leaving.

'Are you sure about this?' he'd kept asking. 'You've prospects here, you know. Give it a couple of years and you could have my job.'

Reggie was touched by this, but he had his explanation worked out.

'No, Mr Hurworth, there's no point in staying. The fact is that the job at the ferry terminal pays more than here, and it's a shorter journey to work. Plus, I get free travel on a staff bus each morning.'

Hurworth was crestfallen.

'But, you're a very valued member of the team, not to mention – and I don't say this lightly – I'm very fond of you, Reggie.'

If only he'd said all of this to me a few months ago, Reggie had thought. Had that been the case, perhaps he'd have been diverted from the plan he'd hatched and would still be an honest man without any of the guilt.

However, Hurworth didn't say it in time, and now Reggie has created the identity of Bobby Grant and left his job at

Littlewoods. All that remains is for him to enact the final phase of the plan. He's arranged to meet Rodney on Thursday, three weeks after the win, in the Magazine, Wallasey.

'Turn up at seven forty-five,' he told him. 'Sit in the bar, not the lounge.'

It was to be just the two of them and not Laura.

It's now 9p.m. on the date in question, and there's still no sign of Rodney. Reggie's first thought is that they've been caught and that the plan had gone awry. He isn't sure what to do. If he goes to Rodney's lodgings in Claughton, he risks being seen by the police, who might have rumbled their scheme. Before leaving, he checks the lounge one last time.

He steps out onto the street, with a wind blowing off the Mersey and rain falling heavily, and he feels utterly miserable. He needs some confirmation that the world is still spinning and, despite the obvious risk, he decides to call Laura at her mother's house.

'Hello?' a woman answers.

'Oh, hello,' Reggie starts, trying to sound suave, sophisticated and educated. 'Would it be possible to speak to Miss Biggs, please?'

'I'm sorry, love,' the voice at the end of the phone says, 'she's gone to London.'

'London?'

'I know! I mean, I'm her mother, and even I was shocked. She's packed her job in, too. Said she wanted to try a different life and to be a success.'

Reggie wants to say, 'But that's not in the bloody plan. She isn't meant to leave her job until next week,' but instead he just hangs up and makes his way, via two buses, back to Woodchurch.

As he enters through the front door, he notices that the kitchen light is on. He walks in and finds Cathy sitting at the table, crying.

'What's the matter?' he asks, without much sympathy in his voice. He is, after all, supposed to be leaving her for a new life with Laura.

'This,' she says, passing him a handwritten note.

It was from Rodney.

Dear Cathy,

Dead sorry, but I have to go away. I can't tell you where. All I can say is that I'll make it up to you, the kids and Reggie. I hope you understand.

'He left this, too,' she wails, indicating what looks to be around three hundred pounds in twenty-pound notes, laid out across the table. 'I'm worried that he's caught up in something!'

Reggie feels the colour draining from his face. He's gone faint. He needs to sit down.

'Bloody hell,' he mutters, almost in tears himself.

'I didn't think you even liked our Rodney,' Cath shouts at him.

This isn't about like or dislike, though. This is the slow realisation that two things have happened. First of all, Rodney has turned the tables and is, in all probability, making off with the entirety of the winnings, but it's the second realisation that causes him pain like he's never experienced before. It's a pain that burns deep into his core and makes him feel like there are no more tomorrows as he understands that his dream of a life with Laura, somewhere new and different, away from the shit of his present stinking hell, is no longer possible.

He glances at the money, which is more than their house has ever seen before, but still so much less than what he knows he should have. It's enough to feed them for three months, but he doesn't want to eat. He doesn't expect that he'll ever eat again. He wants the romance; he wants the excitement of a life with Laura. In his anger, he looks to Cathy.

'Don't spend a penny of that on me, do you hear?'

Cathy looks shocked.

'It's just a gift, Reggie,' she says. 'A gift from our Rodney.'

'It's not a gift,' he shouts. 'It's his way of rubbing our noses in the dirt – his way of showing what a clever bastard he is. I want nothing to do with it.'

He turns, slams the kitchen door and marches upstairs to bed.

*

A week passes without him hearing anything. There's no news from either Rodney or Laura. One evening, while he's talking to Cathy about the Rodney situation, Reggie has a brainwave.

'I'm really worried about what's happening with him,' she's prattling on.

'He'll be fine,' he says flatly.

'But he's never been further than Chester in the past. *London*! I mean, anything could happen to him there.'

Thus, Cathy elaborates on a theory subscribed to by many non-Londoners since time immemorial, that the capital is the most dangerous place in the known world. A city where all imagined horrors and deviance exist, it's the expensive home of not only the wealthy, but also prostitutes, gangsters, spivs and cads. This isn't the London of Primrose Hill, Richmond Riverside, Hyde Park, Barnes and Hampstead. The latter only exist as a place for funny men to go and meet other funny men on the Heath, and by that, people didn't mean Ken Dodd and Arthur Askey.

'Do you want me to try to find him?' Reggie asks, trying his best to come across as caring and sincere.

'Would you know where to look?' Cathy says.

'Well, I've an idea.'

101

'It would be expensive.'

This makes Reggie sigh.

'Is there a price you wouldn't pay to find out that your only brother is safe? Plus, I reckon fifty quid from the money he gave us would cover a week, and it might not even take that long.'

'Would you really do it?'

'You know I would. Of course I would.'

*

Reggie finds himself at Woodside station three days later, catching the train to Paddington. He's wearing his only suit, a double-breasted pinstripe, with a blue shirt and tie. He looks, in his own eyes at least, very smart, but in truth the ensemble isn't nearly as dapper as he imagines. Also, Cathy's constant chain-smoking means that the suit carries the strong scent of stale tobacco, although that was hardly unusual.

He has no idea where Rodney's going to be, but he's certain that he's with Laura, and she's talked constantly about wanting to stay at The Ritz London. It's her life's ambition to order room service, take afternoon tea, walking to Buckingham Palace and luxuriating in a bathroom with golden taps, scented toiletries and the softest towels she's ever encountered. He suspects that's where she and Rodney have headed, and despite knowing that he can't afford to stay there himself, he knows that Paddington Station isn't too far.

He has no photographs of Laura, but he does have one of Rodney, and he hopes that if he shows it to a doorman or a waiter whose palm he crosses with ten shillings, he might make some progress. That's about the only plan he has.

What Reggie fails to anticipate is how intimidating The Ritz would be. The second he enters the lobby, he feels his confidence draining away. A concierge comes across to greet him, and as he does so he glances down at Reggie's shoes. They're Reggie's best pair, but to the flunky they probably look ready for the dustbin.

'Good morning, sir,' the concierge says, 'how may I help you?'

'Erm, I wonder…' Reggie begins before getting momentarily distracted by his own shoes.

He's worried that he's trod in something and can't understand the man's obvious contempt for his footwear.

'Yes, sir?' the man interrupts.

'Erm,' Reggie tries again, suddenly conscious of sounding very Scouse. 'Is there somewhere I can have tea?'

'Are you staying with us, sir?' the flunky asked, milking Reggie's embarrassment to the fullest.

'Erm, no. You know, I just want a cup of tea.'

'And what kind of tea would that be? We have a range, you see.'

'Just normal tea,' Reggie answers firmly, starting to get annoyed with this pompous man.

'English breakfast, sir?'

'No, I've had breakfast. I just want some flipping tea!'

'Sir,' the concierge smirks, 'English breakfast is a type of tea.'

Reggie blushes crimson. 'Well, I knew *that*,' he says, even though clearly, he didn't.

'If sir would like to take a seat…' The concierge points in the direction of a lounge area, near to the check-in desk. 'I will send somebody over to take your order.'

Reggie feels like he's back in Mr Roberts' office again, with this horrible man taking great pleasure in humiliating him. He makes his way over to an armchair and picks up a menu from a nearby table, which he proceeds to glare at without reading anything it says.

A few moments later, a young, pretty Irish waitress comes to take his order.

'Good morning, sir. What can I get you?'

'I just want some tea, love,' Reggie replies glumly.

The girl smiles broadly. 'Oh,' she says, in her Irish brogue, 'you're from Liverpool.'

'I'm not,' said Reggie, 'I'm from Birkenhead. It's a completely different place.'

'Isn't that where the ferry goes to?' she giggles.

'That's right,' he smiles, beginning to feel a bit more comfortable.

'I *love* the Beatles,' she says, rolling her eyes in ecstasy. 'We had them staying with us a few months ago. They were lovely…' She pauses, regaining her decorum. 'Right, I'll fetch you an English Breakfast tea, for one.'

She wanders off and for the first time, Reggie's able to take in the scene around him. It's like nowhere he's been before. The carpet is inches thick, and the seating is soft, luxurious and incredibly clean. There are no jam stains on the arms and no traces of a baby's vomit. Plus, all the ashtrays were clean and empty, despite there being plenty of people smoking.

Our Cathy could learn a thing or two about housekeeping from this place, he thinks.

The waitress reappears, carrying a pot of tea on a silver tray. There's also a small jug of milk and an assortment of rather elaborate-looking biscuits.

'There you are, sir,' she says, reverting to an air of formality, no longer the giggling Beatles fan.

Reggie decides to take his chance.

'I wonder if you can help me,' he says. 'It's a tricky matter, and I need you to be discreet.'

Her interest piqued, she tilts her head to one side.

'Of course, sir. Glad to be of whatever assistance I can.'

He fishes out the picture of Rodney from his wallet.

'Have you seen this man in here recently?'

The word 'recently' is superfluous, he realises, but it's what he hears detectives say on TV.

The girl giggled again.

'Ah, so you know Mr Yardley?'

'Mr Yardley?'

'That's right. That's Mr George Yardley.'

'And he's staying here?'

'Yes,' she answers and then pauses. 'Well, he has been.'

Between the 'yes' and the 'has been', Reggie's hopes soar and then crash down to earth.

'He's not here now?'

'You'll have just missed them. They checked out this morning, him and his lady friend.'

Reggie's pulse quickens again.

'Was she a youngish, pretty brunette?'

'That's right. Her name was Lauren West-Kirby. He was in room 614, and she was across the corridor in 624.'

At least they're not sleeping together, he thinks, wishing he had a photo of Laura, so that he could confirm her identity.

'How old was this woman?' he asks.

'Oh, quite old.'

'Really?'

He's now crestfallen. It isn't her.

'Well, I'd say she was about twenty-nine or thirty, so somewhat older than me.'

It's his turn to smile now.

'That's not old, love; sixty is old.'

'But it's not actually young, either, is it?' she grins.

They must have come down to London to celebrate, he thinks, *and now they're probably heading back north*.

'They seemed very excited,' the girl adds, 'you know, about their new life.'

'How do you mean?' he asks.

'Well, they're off to Australia – headed for the boat at Southampton. Should be leaving around about now.'

Reggie immediately turns ashen.

'Are you alright, sir?'

'No, I'm not. It's very bad news that I've missed them. Could you bring me my bill, please?'

'But you haven't touched your tea.'

'I'll have some in a moment.'

She disappears again, leaving him to contemplate how close he came to catching up with them, and how far away they are now.

For an hour or two, he wanders the streets of London. He passes Buckingham Palace and the Houses of Parliament, and then walks across Westminster Bridge, along the South Bank, to Hungerford Bridge. He ends up in Trafalgar Square, looking up at Nelson atop his column. His mind is empty; his emotions are drained. There's nothing for it, other than to return to Birkenhead.

He catches a bus and heads back to the grotty hotel he'd checked into the night before, and pays his bill before taking the train home. He settles into his first-class compartment, having deliberately chosen one that was empty, and then he falls asleep.

He doesn't wake again until he reaches Woodside. He didn't dream, because his dreams have been shattered, smashed. He steps onto the platform and begins walking towards the bus stop. *Tomorrow*, he thinks, *will be work and drudgery. This is the end of dreaming.*

Cathy's surprised to see him back so soon.

'Did you find him?' she asks earnestly.

'Sort of,' he says. 'I was just a bit late.'

'What do you mean, is he dead?'

'No, love. He's run off to Australia – gone with a woman. The rest, I don't know.'

'*Australia*?' she shrieks. 'But, why?'

'I wish I knew, love.' He shakes his head. 'I really wish I knew.'

This is Reggie's new personal dichotomy. He can't tell anyone about Rodney's good fortune, because he was the perpetrator of the crime. To say anything would be to risk being sent to prison. All he can do is carry on, broken. He has no other choice.

He sleeps fitfully that night, tossing and turning, and running over his stupid mistakes in his head. He's confused by Laura's actions and wonders why she lied to him. Obviously, she and Rodney have established some sort of relationship, but they aren't sleeping together, otherwise they'd have shared a room at The Ritz. What does she see in him? OK, he's handsome and a man of the world, but he's also insincere and unreliable – basically the opposite of Reggie.

Did she string me along the whole time? he asks himself. *Am I a divvy to have believed that we had a future together?*

The night seems endless, but dawn eventually comes. Reggie goes downstairs and turns the gas on, filling the kettle to make tea. It's a cold morning, but he finds himself out in the back garden. He fetches a kitchen chair and sits in the dim half-light with his cup of tea, until he hears baby David crying upstairs, having no doubt filled his nappy with more shit that he'll be expected to clean up. He feels angry, unloved and out of luck. *This isn't Sydney,* he sighs. *This isn't the future.*

*

At times like this, dear reader, we should be grateful that access to guns is restricted in England, because if Reggie had one in his hand, there in the growing light of a chilly spring morning, he would certainly have blown his own brains out. Subsequently, he would have also missed the morning post.

A letter arrives addressed to Reggie. It's marked 'Private & Confidential', in an envelope embossed with The Ritz's livery. It had been posted in Southampton the day before.

Dear Reggie,

I know that you must be hurting. I suspect you're angry, and I can only apologise for the hurt and upset that you're feeling. It was never my intention to betray you, but I couldn't allow you to hurt my sister or your kids, either.

I've always wanted to be straight with you, Reggie. I tried to tell you what was going to happen a few weeks ago, when I suggested that we go to Rovers together. I planned to talk to you about it directly.

The chance didn't crop up, and I'm sorry that I'm now having to do this the coward's way, via a letter, but it's my only option.

The first thing I want you to know is that Laura and I are not romantically involved. She likes me as a friend, not as a lover. You should know, anyway, that I'm not attracted to her or any other woman. That's not my preference, and I'll leave you to work out the rest. We're going to Australia so that we can both start new lives together. Laura, being a good Catholic girl, didn't want it on her conscience that she'd broken up a family. It isn't that she doesn't care about you, or even that she doesn't love you, but she's been racked with guilt at the thought of the harm she was going to inflict upon seven lives – possibly eight, if you include yourself.

This may be hard for you to believe, but I've always seen you as a thoughtful bloke and not nasty in the least. You've always done right by me, and now you've given me the opportunity to escape a suffocating life in Birkenhead and become myself. Please don't judge me on this. It wasn't a personal choice, nor is it a crime. However, it would kill Cathy to know that her brother is a queer, so this has to remain a secret between you and me.

I'm not sure what will happen next, but please don't try to find us. We're on our way to Australia together, but we may go our separate ways once we get there. We haven't decided everything yet. Anyway, as I said, you've always done right by me, and now I want to do right by you.

The payout was £142,000. I have given Laura a third, and enclosed is a cheque for your share, £47,000. This will be honoured by the bank, and I think it should be enough for you and the family to be set for life.

I never wanted to cheat you, and I never wanted you to be harmed. All I want is for you and the family to be happy. Hopefully, this will go some way towards fulfilling that wish.

With sincere best wishes,
Rodney
PS: Up the Rovers!

Reggie has to read the letter several times, as there's too much to comprehend. Also, there's the money. It's a huge amount, enough to pay for houses, education, holidays, food – almost anything, but he knows that it won't buy him the one thing he wants, which is a life with Laura. He's angry at her for not talking this over with him, and he wonders if, given the chance, he could have persuaded her to stick to the plan. Even though in his heart of hearts, he knows he couldn't have changed her mind, he pushes this to the back of his mind, preferring to deceive himself rather than confront the beast that is her resurgent sense of integrity.

Then there's the loot, dear reader, which, adjusted for inflation, amounts to more than half a million in today's money. This is no small sum to a man with no savings, or indeed so much as a bank account of his own. Yet, in his pig-headedness, he's tempted to rip the enclosed cheque into tiny pieces. Luckily, however, he manages to defeat his impetuous impulses.

Finally, there's the shock of it. He never expected Rodney to behave so decently. In his opinion, the man is a scally, a scoundrel and a no-mark, and not for one second did it cross Reggie's mind that his brother-in-law would have enough of a conscience to do the right thing. Then there's the issue of his sexual preferences, about which Reggie had no idea. He always thought of Rodney as a success with the ladies, so to find out that he's a poof is flabbergasting beyond belief. *What next? Would he own up to being an Evertonian, or even a Tory?* Reggie's lack of reference points, having never knowingly met a homosexual before, leave him confused. *Aren't they meant to be camp?* he thinks. *Don't they all dress flamboyantly and wear floppy hats? No, there's something not right about this.*

He's tempted, albeit very briefly, to pick up his coat, take the cheque and run. This would give him the escape he desired. He could leave behind all the crap; all the tedium of Woodchurch, the baby's nappies and the overcooked vegetables. He wouldn't have Laura, but he could probably, given his wealth, find somebody else. *Or I could ignore what Rodney says and go to Australia. I found them once, I could find them again.* The only problem is that it's a big country. He'd guessed lucky with The Ritz after getting lots of clues from Laura beforehand, so it was hardly the work of a genius detective. Also, Australia is too far away. He couldn't just catch a train from Birkenhead Woodside, and there's no guarantee that they'll even be in the same country at the same time. It would be a wild goose chase.

In the back of his mind, Reggie knows two things. First, that his new life was always based upon the idea of being with Laura, and so without her there's nothing. Secondly, he believes, rather pessimistically, in fate. He's not fated to leave his family. He has to stay. Nor is it fated that the family should be wealthy. Cathy wouldn't know what to do with that amount of money, and he suspects that she would fritter it away. He's certain that Laura was his one chance of escape, and that fate has conspired against him, to leave him trapped where he is.

After giving it some more thought, he decides to take the money and put it into a bank account, but instead of going to Birkenhead, he hops on the bus to Chester. There, he looks for a branch of the Trustee Savings Bank, and after talking through what he wants to do with a teller, and having explained that he's depositing a large amount, he's offered the chance to see the branch manager.

'Mr Kellison.' Gareth Whitby, a Welshman with reddish hair, greets him with a firm handshake. 'Please, come and join me in my office, and take a seat. Now, how may I help you?'

For some reason, Reggie is close to tears.

'I want to open a bank account,' he says. 'I've come into some money, and I want it to be put away safely for my children.'

'So, do you want a cheque account or a deposit account? And exactly how much is it that you're putting in?'

'I've never had a bank account before, so I need your help

choosing an account,' Reggie says sheepishly before pausing for a moment. 'And the amount is forty-seven thousand pounds.'

Gareth Whitby gasps. 'That is a very large sum of money, Mr Kellison.'

'Yes,' Reggie agrees.

'Will you be wanting to make regular withdrawals?'

'No, I want it to be put aside for when my kids come of age. There are six of them.'

'I see. In which case, I think you'll need a unit trust.'

'What's that?'

'It's a tax-efficient way of saving, which also grows over time.'

'The thing is, I want to give this money anonymously. I don't want them to know that it came from me.'

'OK, and how much do you want to put into this fund?'

'All of it.'

'Really, Mr Kellison? Surely you want to use some of the money for yourself and your good wife?'

'No. Absolutely not.'

Whitby again looks shocked.

'Very well,' he nods, adding to the notes he's been taking as they went along. 'This is a very large sum of money, Mr Kellison. You'll be our biggest single depositor by some distance. I need to go through some paperwork with you, and you will, of course, have me as your personal account manager.'

'OK,' Reggie responds, not realising the importance or significance of this statement.

'Will it be yourself and your wife who will act as signatories?'

'No, just me. My wife is never to know about this.'

'And how often would you like bank statements?'

Reggie doesn't know what a bank statement is. Once it's been explained to him, he asks, 'Can I just come in and collect them?'

'We normally send them by post, on a monthly basis.'

'I won't need them that often. I'll come and collect them myself every three months.'

Whitby raises an eyebrow but dutifully notes down the requirements.

'Could I have a telephone number to reach you on?'

'Telephone?' Reggie laughs bitterly. 'We can't afford a telephone.'

Whitby is visibly bewildered.

It takes another forty minutes to complete all the necessary paperwork, and then Reggie leaves the bank knowing that he's done exactly the right thing. For his part, Whitby has a great story to tell down at the golf club when he retires, about the strange man with a huge amount of money and no telephone.

Reggie begins to feel as though he has, to an extent, achieved what could be called a degree of closure. There's little doubt that he'd been haunted by what he'd intended to do, and he's now come around to thinking that the best course of action is to accept his responsibilities as a father. The money he's set aside will ensure that his kids are all looked after, and that they will get a good start in life.

As for Laura, well, no amount of philanthropy is going to cure Reggie's broken heart. From time to time, he remembers her smile, her hair and even her perfume, but with each passing day, the actual memory of her fades until she becomes an emotion, not a person. She's a source of melancholia, regret and sadness, but eventually her face becomes harder to recall. Her voice, however, is a different matter. He never forgets the clarity of her voice, its playfulness and the sheer joy he got from listening to her speak. In the end, his forgetting is more painful than the memory ever was. Forgetting means that it's possible to imagine that the whole thing was simply a long, exceptionally vivid dream.

What about you, dear reader? Are there parts of your life that now feel like a dream? Lovers you've lost, faces that have faded and moments of passion extinguished. Did you choose to forget them, because the pain of recollection is just too much, or could it be that your imagination has tricked you, and none of those memories are actually your own? Maybe none of those events that make you whimsical or melancholy ever happened. There is, after all, such a thing as false memories.

In that regard, you and Reggie may not be so different. Of course, you've probably never stolen large amounts of money or considered abandoning your family for a younger lover, although if you have, well, you'll know exactly the kind of hurt that Reggie's feeling. If you haven't committed such sins, have you ever thought, *isn't it time I let go of my fear? Isn't it time I stopped hiding in the shadows, and instead felt the warmth of the sun's rays melting away my misery, my frustrations and my longings?*

Who knows, in pursuing these ideals, you may discover a part of you that *is* a little bit devilish. The part of you who waits in line with eleven items at the ten-item till, and who parks in a disabled parking bay when you have no ailment to speak of. There could even be a part of you who stares across at a colleague in the workplace, dreaming of something better than the misery you go home to each evening.

You see, you're now in Reggie's world, like it or not.

Rodney likes Australia, and he likes Australians.

The country is young. It feels energetic and forward-focused. England, by comparison, is old-fashioned, and even with Wilson as Prime Minister, there's a sense that the old guard still runs the place. There's simply too much deference, to the queen, the BBC, *The Times*, and to all the other pillars who prop up the establishment. There's more to life than cricket at Lords or the Henley Royal Regatta.

Life is different down under. The weather is either good or great, the beer is cheap and delicious, and the people he meets are straight-talking and honest. There's very little to not like, and much to put a smile on your face, like the ferries across Sydney Harbour, cricket at the Sydney Cricket Ground and surfing on Manly Beach. Rodney loves everything about his new city, his new home. When he gets bored, he travels, to Adelaide, to Melbourne or to Brisbane. All the cities he visits fascinate him. He loves the Gold Coast in Brisbane, with its long sweep of beaches and laid-back pace, although Sydney itself isn't particularly frantic. There's a feeling that every day is a day for partying.

He occasionally takes Laura with him to Brisbane, and they pose as a married couple, Mr and Mrs Yardley, usually hiring a well-heeled apartment overlooking the shoreline. He goes to Melbourne alone, though.

Melbourne is his secret playground, his Xanadu. He never takes Laura there, because that's where he goes for real satisfaction. When he first arrived, he was only confident using saunas, but there he was able to meet handsome, fit young men, who he could take back to his hotel and enjoy. As time went by, and he built a network of mates, he began to explore the emerging underground gay clubs, and as the sixties gave way to the seventies, the scene became less underground and more open, albeit with 'queer-bashing' gangs always being a risk. He occasionally returns to Sydney with a bruised face and torso, but compared to life in Liverpool, it's Heaven.

He doesn't need to work, but he wants his investments to deliver a return. He bought a couple of retail units near Sydney Harbour, and after these did well he increased his portfolio to a dozen. He managed to get in before the boom happened, and since everybody now wants to be down at the harbour as

Sydney establishes itself as a tourist destination, his properties all rake in decent profits.

His marriage to Laura is one of convenience. They don't actually live together, but they often share a dinner table, and if he stays at her place, he sleeps in the spare room. It always reminds him of their time at The Ritz, with her sleeping across the hall from him, excited and companionable but always clear about her boundaries. In all of their time together, they've never once seen each other naked, as it was neither necessary nor appropriate, and if they kissed, it was only ever on the cheek.

To the outside world, their relationship seems amicable, kind and built on trust. They have few real friends, but a number of associates, and if you ask any of those people to describe them as a couple, they'll use such terms as 'fun', 'lively' or 'friendly'. They never refer to them as anything approaching passionate, however, and rarely is there a mention of love.

Luckily, Rodney doesn't really care what people think. He's comfortable in his new life, and those he meets when he's out with Laura are neither people he's out to impress nor offend. If ever the conversation steers towards questions about children, they have their script prepared. 'We can't have them,' they explain, and then they use the embarrassment this usually causes the enquirer to change the subject swiftly.

Is he happy? Absolutely! Does he miss anything about his old life? Only the obvious things, like going to Prenton Park, or decent English beer, proper Scouse humour and his family. If you push him further, he also misses having a history. In Sydney, there are no points of personal reference; no pubs he drank in when he was underage and no corners where a half-fumbled passion had ended in disappointment. Yet, these are all minor drawbacks, with the one exception being family.

He has one sister, Cathy, and even though he was never particularly close to her, he adores his nephews and nieces.

To him, they represent hope for the future, and he's especially proud that Barry went off and trained to become a teacher. In fact, he's totally enamoured with all of their potential, right down to baby David, who he reckoned must be coming up to seven now. All six of them have the opportunity to write a new story for the future.

Then there's the kids' father. Rodney knows how much he irritated Reggie, but he's always been quite fond of his brother-in-law. Plus, and this was a big plus, he owes him a debt. Without Reggie, there would be no Australian adventure; without Reggie, there would be no life with Laura to act as his foil; and without Reggie, he'd still be the same old scally, ducking and diving to make ends meet.

He wants to know that Reggie has put his share of the money to good use. He hopes that he's bought a big house, that he's learned to drive and got himself a car, and that the kids get to go on exciting holidays. A holiday for Reggie and his family had meant booking a week off work and going on coach trips to the Lake District, North Wales or York. Now, however, they should at the very least be able to afford a few weeks in Benidorm. Finally, he hopes that Reggie has bought himself a season ticket for Rovers. He's heard that a new Main Stand has been built, and he imagines that the facilities will be an upgrade on the old, rickety wooden one it's replaced. He wants all the good things in life to happen for Reggie.

All of this means that his curiosity will inevitably get the better of him, and that he'll find a way to write home and check how things are going.

Yet, dear reader, *we* know that Reggie has already sacrificed short-term gain and his own personal comfort for the long-term benefit of his children.

When Barry turned twenty-one, he received a cheque in

the post for £12,370, and while this may not seem much to you, dear reader, it was the equivalent of around a hundred and fifty thousand.

'Dad! Dad! Look!' the birthday boy had yelled excitedly as he entered the kitchen one October afternoon.

'What is it?' Reggie asked.

'Somebody's given me a whopping load of cash,' Barry said, showing his father the cheque. 'It's weird, though. It came with a letter that says, "It's a condition of the bequest that you only spend the money on yourself, and not the immediate Kellison family."'

'Really?' Reggie acted surprised. 'Well, that's interesting, isn't it?'

They were soon joined by Cathy.

'Look, Mum,' Barry said before repeating the story.

'That'll be our Rodney,' Cathy declared. 'Heart of gold, our Rodney.'

'Do you think?' Reggie asked. 'I'm not so sure.'

He knew that there was no point in seeking credit, even though he was hurt that Cathy would assume that the only person in the world who'd give the family money was her deadbeat brother.

'It's obvious,' she said, 'unless you and Fred have a fancy woman you haven't told us about.'

The look of contempt on Cathy's face wounded Reggie to the core. He hated her maliciousness. In fact, he hated her in general, but he felt he owed it to his kids to put up with her.

'So, what are we going to spend it on?' she asked.

'The letter says it can only be spent by our Barry,' Reggie said sharply. 'Isn't that right, son?'

'That's what it says, Dad,' Barry confirmed.

'How would they know who spent it?' Cathy asked.

'Are you mad?' Reggie said. 'What if they did find out, and Barry had to give it all back?'

He gave his wife a look that tried to convey the message, *keep your grubby little hands off my son's money.*

'Well,' Barry said, 'I won't use *this* money, but I'm taking you for a pint, Dad, alright?'

'That would be smashing, son,' Reggie smiled.

'And what about me?' Cathy quizzed.

'I start that job in Kent in a few weeks, so when I get paid, I can send you some money and still keep to the conditions in the letter.'

'Typical,' Cathy sighed. 'It's just like my brother to make sure I don't get a penny.'

Reggie didn't reveal the truth. For Cathy, the truth would always be a foreign country, a land she'd never visit, or even receive a postcard from.

*

Around the time of Barry's twenty-first birthday, Rodney's compelled to visit a solicitor's office in downtown Sydney. He isn't sure who to go to, but he finds a listing for a Gertrude Millington, whose strapline in the Yellow Pages included the phrase 'discretion assured', and he reckons she could be just what he's after.

He expects an old lady, maybe somebody approaching retirement, and is quite taken aback to discover that far from being all musty or smelling of lavender, Ms Millington is tall, leggy and stunningly attractive. Hers is the sort of beauty that seems effortless and would turn heads on any street, boasting a figure that could best be described as vaguely pornographic. Even for a man of Rodney's persuasion, it's difficult not to get excited in her presence.

119

'Mr Yardley,' she says as he enters her office. 'Pleased to meet you. How may I be of service?'

She wears a pair of reading glasses on a silver chain around her neck, and as she makes no move to put them on, Rodney wonders if perhaps she keeps them to hand just in case a man she's talking to is finding her face too mesmerising. He begins to explain his situation, and he tells her that he wants to find a way to communicate with his family back in the UK without them being able to trace him.

'May I ask why?' she asks.

Rodney has already planned his response.

'I can't go into details, but it's all legal and above board.'

She looks at him carefully, as if weighing him up.

'OK, let's run through your options.'

Eventually, Ms Millington comes up with a scheme whereby any letter sent or responded to would go through her office. She has links with a firm in San Francisco, so, for the sake of smokescreening, some of the letters would be sent from there. They agree that her PA will call him whenever any correspondence is received, and that they'll initially aim to deal with twelve letters per year, six each way.

As he's leaving, Rodney can't help but comment on how Ms Millington is so much different than how he imagined.

'My dad was a Lancashire cow farmer with a penchant for traditional family names,' she laughs. 'He once said to me, "Gertrude, if you ever go anywhere near a cow, I'll have you murdered!" So, I became a lawyer, moved out here and the rest, as they say, is all surprises.'

Rodney smiles. It isn't often he's charmed by a woman, much less a lawyer, but Gertrude just has something about her.

Writing his first letter home, he decides to keep it light.

Dear Reggie,

I hope this letter finds you well and that all is good with the family.

I just wanted to let you know that I'm doing great. I'm enjoying my new life and I've started to make a success of it.

Moving abroad was the best thing I ever did. It gave me a new lease of life in a place where nobody knew me, bar one person.

I did right by you, and I hope that over the past few years you've been able to move the family forwards. I'm writing to your address on Caldwell Drive, but I expect that you've moved to a new house by now. I'm sure that the GPO will find a way of making sure this letter gets to you.

How are the kids? Has Barry graduated yet? Does he have a job?

Any letter you send needs to go to the address shown in the cover letter attached. I'm never in one place very long, but my solicitor will always find a way of getting it to me, if you respond.

Warmest regards,
Rodney
PS: What's the new stand like at Rovers?

He's reviewed the letter two or three times. He knows he needs to get the balance right – he can't be too aggressive or too passive – but he also suspects that he may never get a response, anyway. That would make crafting it a bit pointless in some respects, like painting a picture that would never be put on display, but still he sends the letter and waits.

At first, Reggie's bewildered by the letter he receives from

Rodney, not least because the covering note is full of jargon and instructions for how to respond. He finds this intimidating, and it almost gets in the way of him even considering a response.

He isn't sure what to do. The pain of losing Laura is beginning to subside, like a toothache that you never bother to get fixed. Most of the time you don't notice it, but then you're out walking, or you see a customer passing through the turnstiles at Woodside, and suddenly all the aches and suffering are right there in front of you. In the beginning, it often left him feeling down for days on end, but as time progressed this became less acute. He still gets the occasional sharp jolt, though, as a reminder that there was once the opportunity for life to be better.

He thinks carefully before he responds. *Is there any point?* he wonders. *Does Rodney just want to gloat about his new life?* He drafts several versions of a reply, most of which he knows are too aggressive. Early examples include:

Dear Rodney,

You have some cheek, don't you? Have you not thought about how much pain you've caused me...?

Dear Rodney,

Why have you now decided to write to me? I think you're the lowest of the low...

Dear Rodney,

Not content with taking Laura away from me, it seems that you now want to rub my nose in the dirt...

All of these openings and points are true reflections of Reggie's hurt and anger at what his brother-in-law has done, but they aren't really him. He knows that there's no reason why Rodney should have sent the money when he did, and that while Reggie himself wouldn't benefit from it, his kids definitely would. For this, he has to thank Rodney.

After various drafts, he settles on this:

Dear Rodney,

I was a bit taken aback to hear from you. Since you walked off with Laura, I've been a bit lost, and I've only recently started to see the world a bit more coherently. Not all of this is down to you, but I would have thought, given your disposition, you would have had a bit more sensitivity to my own situation.

Not much here has changed. I'm still working at Woodside, and we're still living in Caldwell Drive, albeit we're moving to a bigger house in the next few weeks. This will be at Ferny Brow Road, and now that Barry has left home, it means that everyone apart from the three youngest will have their own room.

I'm grateful that you gave me a share of your winnings. I've invested it all into a trust fund for the kids, which will pay out when each of them turns twenty-one. As you may remember, Barry has just come of age, so he has a nice little nest egg that will help to set him up going forward. It's another seventeen years until David comes of age, but hopefully the pot will grow enough so that each of the kids gets the same amount of money, in terms of value, as the others. Cathy thinks the money came from you, which I suppose is sort of true, so you're still getting credit where none is due.

As for Rovers, I haven't been in the new stand yet. It's gigantic, but I prefer the popular side of the ground on Borough Road. We were doing great until Yardley got injured at Shrewsbury, and then our season went belly-up.

It's been hard writing this letter, though I'm not sure why. I know that you wish me no harm, but I constantly wonder what my life could have been like if we'd done what we said we'd do. I'm not angry or sad about this, just curious.

Take care,

Reggie

Rodney is flabbergasted by Reggie's letter. *What the hell is he doing?* he thought. *Why is he still working at the ferries? Why haven't they left Caldwell Drive yet?* He writes back immediately:

Dear Reggie,

A short note, but seriously, I don't understand it. Why haven't you made better choices? That money could have set you up for life.

I think you've made a big mistake. You and my sister could be so much happier.

Rodney

Reggie's response is equally short:

Dear Rodney,

This scheme was never intended to make life better for Cathy and me. Cathy played no part in my thinking, Laura did, and she's with you now, not me. The way I see things, there were no strings attached to the money, and I'm simply doing right by my kids.

I've never hankered after money for the sake of having it. In fact, if I really think about it, which I do a great deal, I think money has become the biggest part of the problem. We were hypnotised by thoughts of our lives changing beyond recognition. Well, mine did change, but not in the way I wanted.

Think about it, and then you'll realise that it makes perfect sense.

Reggie

Again, Rodney responds instantly:

Reggie,

Money may not make you happy, but poverty can make you sad, ill and old beyond your years.

This money has allowed me to become the person I always wanted to be. I think it's great that you're putting your kids first, but have a heart for Cathy, please.

As for Laura, she's clear. There was no real prospect of a life with you. She liked you, cared about you and even loved you a little, but not enough to break up your family. Stop dreaming, Reggie. You're being daft.

Rodney

Some of what Rodney wrote strikes a chord with Reggie. He knows that struggling to make ends meet isn't conducive to good health. Indeed, his physical state hasn't been great for the past few months. It's nothing in particular, but he always seems to feel tired and lacking in energy. Having said that, with overtime bonuses and shift allowances, he's earning more at the ferries than he was at Littlewoods. Plus, now that Barry has left home, there's once less mouth to feed.

Soon, Lynn and Vaughan will also be working, so he knows that if he can carry on earning like he has been for a few months longer, there will be light at the end of the tunnel.

Dear Rodney,

I never had the chance to talk to Laura, so I've no idea if you're telling the truth or not.

I made a decision that Cathy wouldn't get any of the money. What would she do with it? She'd probably waste it on rubbish. This way, I make sure that the kids reap all the benefits. That can't be a bad thing, can it? My biggest worry was that with Cathy, the money would be gone quickly. I think you'll see that there's method to my madness.

As for working, unlike you, I've always liked earning an honest wage from honest work. It's a simple maxim, don't you think?

Reggie

Dear Reggie,

It genuinely makes me sad to think of you not having the life you could. I bet you're working some stinking shifts in that job at the ferries – earlies, lates, the lot.

It's your choice. You're too noble, and you know it. Nobility is a good thing among the toffs and the like, but for us ordinary people it sometimes means that we end up missing out – always eating the crumbs from the table and never being at the feast.

I'm actually making an honest living now without having to work too hard. Yes, back home I was a bit of a scoundrel, always on the rob or diddling the taxman out of a bob or two, but that's in the past. Now, I'm an honest and upright citizen, paying my way and contributing taxes.

Your choice, Reggie, but I still think it's a daft one.

Rodney

One afternoon, Reggie returns from work to find Cathy sitting at the kitchen table, smoking and reading the letters. He thought he'd hidden them well at the back of the top of a wardrobe, but obviously not well enough.

'Who's Laura?' she demands, eyes aflame.

'Sorry?' he asks, feigning ignorance.

'*Laura*!' she screams. 'You must know her, because you were planning on leaving us all for her!'

As he stares down at his shoes, Cathy gets up from the table and grabs him by the hair.

'You fucking tell me who and where she is!'

'I don't know,' he splutters, feeling the pain in his scalp increase as she tightens her grip.

'You don't know? You don't know, but you were planning to fuck off with her?'

'I don't know *where* she is.'

'So, you don't deny you were going to leave, you pathetic bag of shite! I've given you six kids – eight if you count the two that miscarried – and you, you snivelling little arsehole, were planning to walk away from me and them!'

The argument raged for a good hour, until Cathy, who was usually a woman of few words, finally ran out of insults to throw at Reggie.

'I'm off to see a priest,' she spat, grabbing her coat and storming out of the kitchen. 'You can sort tea out. I don't know when or if I'll be back!'

As he walks back from the chippy with a fish supper for the kids and him, part of Reggie is relieved that some of the truth was out in the open. However, he's less pleased about the barrage of questions he faces as soon as he walks through the front door.

'Why isn't Mum here?' little Reg asks.

'When will she be home?' Kay follows.

As for David, he just cries relentlessly.

It's well after the kids have gone to bed when Cathy returns, just as Reggie is about to turn in himself. He's on a six–two tomorrow and has to be up at 5a.m.

'You're sleeping on the settee,' she tells him, and he knows her well enough to understand that this is non-negotiable.

It's the last thing he needs before an early shift, but he accepts his fate with the same sense of resignation that a man waiting for the gallows might display.

In the middle of the night, Vaughan, who's not the sharpest knife in the block, comes down for a glass of water.

'Why are you on the couch?' he asks, shaking Reggie awake.

The best Reggie can muster is a half-hearted, 'Go back to sleep, son. Everything's okay.'

At work the following morning, Reggie is bleary-eyed and bad-tempered after almost missing the staff bus. He returns from his mid-morning tea break and is surprised to be called into the superintendent's office, where he's even more surprised to find two police officers waiting for him.

'Reggie,' the superintendent says solemnly, 'I'm afraid there's some terrible news. Please, take a seat.'

Reggie immediately fears the worse. *Cath must have figured out where the money came from and then told the police*, he thought.

'Hello, Mr Kellison,' the first officer says, 'I'm Sergeant Foulkes from the Upton station. You're the husband of Catherine Kellison, is that correct?'

'That's right,' Reggie confirms.

'I'm afraid your wife is dead, sir,' Sergeant Foulkes says, bowing his head.

Reggie is stunned. He can feel his bottom lip quivering and his eyes welling with tears.

'How?' he just about manages to ask.

'It seems she stepped out in front of a bus, sir. We think it might have been suicide, as witnesses stated that she looked straight at the driver as she did it. She was killed instantly. There would have been no suffering.'

Reggie begins to sob very, very loudly as Fred appears in the doorway.

'Mr Hughes is going to take you home, Reggie,' his supervisor says softly. 'Take as long as you need. We'll continue to pay you in full until you come back.'

Fred, who's obviously been made aware of what's happened, wraps an enormous arm around Reggie's shoulder.

'Come on, son,' he says quietly, 'let's get you home.'

The next few days are a blur, and all Reggie can think about is keeping the letters secret. If they're discovered, there's a risk that he might go to prison, which would mean the money being sequestrated and the kids put into care. It feels as if the world has stopped spinning. The Prague Spring is coming to an end, Ho Chi Minh is winning in Vietnam, and Reggie's world seems to be on the verge of collapse. This being 1968, doctors won't prescribe him tranquillisers. Instead, men are expected to remain stoic. The only available medicine is alcohol, and thus he and Fred spend a great deal of time in the pub, while Dot virtually moves into Caldwell Drive to look after the shell-shocked children.

'I wish I could have done more,' Reggie mutters one night in The Pelican, a pub on the Woodchurch Estate.

'You did loads,' Fred said. 'You gave her six lovely kids. You've worked hard all your life. You were loyal, kind and—'

'It's all a lie,' Reggie cuts him off. 'I failed her, Fred. I failed her dreadfully, and she knew, and she—'

Fred throws his hands up to stem the tide.

'You need a whisky, Reggie. I'll get you one.'

While Fred's at the bar, Reggie manages to regain some of his composure. He begins to feel in control again, but then a few moments later Barry walks into the pub and heads straight for his dad, throwing his arms around him in a long, slow bear hug. He's just arrived back from Kent, where he'd been working.

'Dad,' Barry croaks through streaming tears, 'I am so, so sorry.'

They're both sobbing now, and Fred, being the caring, observant kind of guy he is, clocks the scene and asks for an extra whisky. He gives Barry a nod as he hands out the glasses, which are downed in one, and then without comment or question, he returns to the bar and orders three more.

'Does Rodney know?' Barry eventually asks.

'There's no way of contacting him, son,' Reggie lies. 'He could be anywhere in the world. How would we find him?'

Barry thinks for a moment.

'Couldn't we check through the bank? You know, they must know, since that's where my birthday money came from.'

'I'm not sure that's where the money came from,' Reggie lies again. 'That was just your mum's assumption.'

'Well, it would be a start,' Barry says pleadingly.

In truth, Reggie has already written to Rodney. It was a short note:

Dear Rodney,

Terrible news, I'm afraid. Cathy's dead. She was run over by a bus a few days ago.

I know this letter won't reach you before the funeral takes place next week at Landican, but I thought you should know nevertheless.

She was always very proud of you, believing that you'd made a success of your life since you went abroad. I know that she loved you dearly.

130

Everybody's very upset here, as you can imagine. I'm not at all sure what happens next.

Sincerely,

Reggie

He has no idea how Rodney will react to his sister's death. However, he knew that Rodney wouldn't return to England for a host of reasons, not least the possibility of his past catching up with him.

The funeral itself is restricted to close friends and family. There's a requiem mass, where words are said that mean little and tears are shed that mean far more. Shortly after the coroner's report is concluded, Cathy's death is recorded as 'misadventure', but Reggie knows that it was more like a murder.

Rodney's devastated when he hears of his sister's death, and his grief is compounded by the fact that he knows the ceremony would be over with before he could hope to get back to England. In the modern world, we'd call it 'having a problem with closure', but in 1968, he's simply a man who isn't coping very well.

Laura had an immediate worry of her own. She's concerned that Reggie will see this as a perfect excuse to leave England and try to find her. She has no idea that Rodney and Reggie have been in touch, which is just as well, as even allowing for the elaborate arrangements that Rodney had put in place, there's still the possibility that they could be tracked down. It wouldn't take a genius to join the dots, and while Reggie's naive, he isn't stupid. He'd piece things together sooner or later.

She likes the freedom she has in Australia. She's never really wanted kids, fearing that they'd become a burden to her, especially with Rodney's sexual preferences making him a less than ideal father. She's now used to taking lovers almost at will. She sleeps with older men, younger men and has occasionally even slept with the odd woman. However, unlike her husband, she has no real interest in same-sex relations. The first couple of times were a novelty, but not really her cup of tea. She can only really be satisfied by a man, and if Reggie appears on the scene, he'll prevent her from pursuing her secret pastimes.

There's a period of waiting, but no news arrives from England. As each day passes, she becomes more and more convinced that it's only a matter of time before Reggie and his kids appear on her doorstep.

While Reggie has entertained the idea of making a fresh start somewhere new in the wake of Cathy's death, he hasn't considered trying to find Laura. As far as he's concerned, she rejected him, so why would he want to pursue her? There's also the issue of his children, with Reg, Kay and David all still at school, leaving him little time to plan an exciting future.

It's roughly two months after Cathy's funeral, when he receives another letter from Rodney:

Dear Reggie,

I'm devastated. It's taken all the strength I can summon to get through the past few weeks. Cathy, dead? It's like being told that Tranmere no longer exist.

I wonder now if you regret not using the money to give the two of you a better life. Don't you think that would have made her happier, having at least a couple of years to enjoy her wealth? I think what you've done borders on cruelty. Actually, no, let me revise that. I *know* what you've done is cruel, selfish and even wicked.

I'm wondering, though, how are the kids coping? Are they OK? Is there anything they need that I can help with?

I'm sorry. I know some of this sounds harsh. I'm just up in the air.

Thinking about you and the kids.

Rodney

Reggie's very angry after reading Rodney's missive. In part, this is because the truth is like dental treatment without the anaesthetic – it always hurts. It's also incredibly insensitive, as Rodney must surely understand the guilt that Reggie's feeling; it wouldn't take a genius to work it out. Plus, the stuff about the kids has annoyed him. Reggie doesn't need Rodney's charity.

Dear Rodney,

I found your letter very upsetting.

I did my best by Cathy, as I've done my best by the kids. I don't need your charity.

It might be better if we stop corresponding now.

Take care,

Reggie

*

That was their final correspondence. Rodney did write a few more times, but Reggie binned the letters without opening them.

There were, therefore, only four letters for Barry and David to work with. Would you not say that they were searching for a needle in a haystack, dear reader? Is it not highly unlikely that they'll ever make contact with Rodney or Laura? Has Reggie passed on his disposition towards optimism to his children, or are they just as stupid as their father? We shall see.

Why does life happen and yet not happen? How is it that we go through our days in a haze, a state of dazed stupidity, rather than being fully alert? The Buddhists argue that until we learn to meditate, and are thus able to look into our bodies from the outside, this will always be the case.

It's fair to say that both Reggie and Rodney spend time in spiritual purgatory following Cathy's death. Neither is fully aware of what's going on around him, and they're each overcome by the blinding, eating grief of a guilty conscience. They both, for different reasons, believe that they had, and squandered, the power to correct the errors of the world and heal the wounds of the sins committed against the transgressed.

They are, of course, both wrong. Their beliefs are, to put it politely, somewhat primitive, and if we're not worrying about politeness, we might describe them as a little egocentric. It's impossible for one or two acts of kindness to cleanse a soul of the sins that have transgressed it. It could be argued that this flawed idea is the lie upon which Catholicism rests, that by will alone we can cast aside any evil we've committed, but in truth, life is not so forgiving. Men such as Stalin, Hitler or Pol Pot can never have been absolved of their crimes against humanity through a sudden conversion to piety, so why should it be any different for Reggie or Rodney? No amount of Mass or confession is going to lift them from where they find themselves.

'I wonder how Reggie's doing,' Rodney often asks.

'He'll be fine,' Laura always replies, 'you know that.'

'I hope so.'

Rodney says this in the same way you might suggest that a stray cat could decide to return, or that a lost set of door keys would eventually just turn up. The truth is, neither he nor

Laura really knows. The words they exchange are of comfort, not conviction.

It reminds this writer that we're all basically the same. After the 9/11 tragedy, there were few families wandering around Lower Manhattan, telling people that their deceased loved ones were in fact horrible pieces of work. In much the same vein, no one can bring themselves to acknowledge that a significant contributor to the Kellison family's misery back in Birkenhead was Cathy's poor stewardship of her marriage. The phrase 'don't speak ill of the dead' encourages one to ignore the fact that Cathy was a less than perfect wife, and you, dear reader, will doubtless recall situations where death has somehow airbrushed a person's sins from history.

For several months, Rodney ceases visiting Melbourne and Laura puts her sexual conquests on hold. They find themselves spending more time in each other's company, in an unconscious attempt to offer support through a kind of platonic tenderness. They take holidays, travelling to New Zealand, Fiji, California and Singapore, and they genuinely enjoy each other's company. They each appreciate the understanding of the other, since they alone know the truth of how they came to be where they are. Other couples talk about meeting at parties or cricket matches, or even being introduced by mutual friends. Rodney and Laura's foundations, on the other hand, were more embarrassing than meeting through an agency, or by swiping right on Tinder. Consider what your reaction would be to the following conversation:

'So, how did you two meet?' you ask.

They both glance down at the floor for a moment until Laura moves her hair back from her face, smiles and says, 'Well, it's complicated.'

Rodney gives a nervous cough, but you won't be thrown off that easily.

'I'm all ears,' you say with an encouraging smile and an enthusiastic nod.

'Honestly?' Laura asks, warming to her task.

'Absolutely,' you reply, keen to learn the truth.

Laura sighs at this point, but when Rodney tries to interrupt, she shows him the palm of her hand and begins.

'We were partners in crime,' she says, a mischievous half-smile spreading across her lips.

'Oh, come on, be serious,' you playfully admonish.

'I *am* being serious,' she insists, fixing you with a stare while Rodney squirms in the seat next to her. 'We stole a huge amount of money and then ran away together.'

How do you react? Do you laugh nervously, call the police, or simply disassociate yourself from this pair of weirdos and their warped sense of humour?

Their official line, by the way, is that Rodney's brother-in-law, who used to work with Laura, introduced them. It's sort of the truth, but not the whole of it. You do this yourself, don't you? 'Sort of the truth' is a softer currency to trade in than gold-backed honesty. 'Sort of the truth' is the microwave meal that's more expensive than buying raw ingredients but involves little effort. It's masturbating to porn rather than making love to someone, and it's watching a football match on fast forward, so that you just see the goals without having to sit through the tedium of a live game. In the modern world, we've become addicted to half-truths, quarter-truths and outright lies.

Reggie's never going to take up meditation. Like most men, with the notable exception of The Fab Four, he sees such behaviour as indulgent, if not weird. Besides, he worships at the temple of Prenton Park, using occasional visits to the Super White Sangha to get him back on an even keel.

Life is hard as a lone parent, but he knows that there's no alternative. A nagging thought hangs at the back of his mind, suggesting that God has punished him with Cathy's death. It isn't that he loved her, but he did need her. Now, his days are filled with dashes to the supermarket and pre-cooking meals, which the newly promoted Kay serves for tea (not dinner) for Reg, David and herself after school. It's actually working well, with Kay growing in confidence in her new role, even though at the age of twelve she's still too young to be a housewife. The punishing God had made Reggie's life more chaotic, but at the same time, he reasons, it's removed a major source of unhappiness. It's only David who seems unable to grasp the reality of the situation.

'When's Mum coming home?' the little boy asks pleadingly.

'I've already explained it to you, son.' Reggie sighs and puts down his paper. 'She's not coming home. She died.'

'Why did she die?' he asks, his big blue eyes a picture of innocence.

'She got run over, remember?'

'I know that. I just don't know *why* she had to die.'

Reggie comforts David, absorbing the tremors that shake his tiny body as once again he begins to sob. At just five years old, the boy cannot process the randomness of the world. All he's ever experienced is the love of his family, and while Reggie knows that his pain will lessen over time, he hates the fact that he's at least partly responsible for his child's despair. *Maybe one day he'll hate me for what I've done*, he thinks.

It won't be one day soon, but maybe one day.

*

From: Tranmere-boy-down-under
To: BJ Kellison
Date: 6 February 2005

Alright Bazza,

I got the letters, but to me they don't make much sense without the stuff Dad wrote. Still, I think the following *might* be true:

Rodney is gay.

Dad had the hots for this Laura woman in a big way.

Dad, not Rodney, is responsible for the money we all got at twenty-one.

Rodney, for whatever reason, seems angry at Mum's death.

If you think I'm going to hang around gay bars in Kings X looking for him, you can think again! I reckon the best way to find him is to find this Laura woman. Looking for Rovers supporters in random sports bars is going to deliver sod all!

Three draws on the trot now! Are we as bad as we seem?

David

From: BJ Kellison
To: Tranmere-boy-down-under
Date: 8 February 2005

David,

We're even worse than we seem, make no mistake. With the money and support we have, we should be doing much better than this. Rumour has it that PJ just isn't putting the dosh in.

I think you might be right about finding Laura and not Rodney. Intuitively, I suspect that she'll be somewhat easier to locate, simply because there are likely to be fewer women from Liverpool in Sydney. Don't hang out in gay bars – too risky, and we don't need to take risks like that. Knowing you, you'll end up coming home HIV positive!

You only have until the end of the month, and you need a holiday, so don't waste too much time on this.

From: Tranmere-boy-down-under
To: BJ Kellison
Date: 10 February 2005

Bazza,

I could only be HIV positive if I let someone fuck me – not going to happen!

If I get close to finding either one of them, I might extend my stay, but that's a big *if* in my book. As it is, I'm heading off to Melbourne for a few days at the weekend. There are a couple of gigs I want to see, and I also want to check out the talent. Meant to be cracking!

Back in touch in about five days.

David.

PART 3

'Better do a good deed near at home than go far away to burn incense'

Amelia Earhart

It would be fair to say that David Kellison is having a great time in Australia. He likes the beer, the women and the people; he likes the sun being out each day, the club scene and the way everyone seems to be smiling all the time. It's brilliant, even better than he'd imagined, and his only regret is not having come sooner.

He kind of knows that he's on a wild goose chase, and he and Barry have already discussed how much time he should spend trying to track down Rodney. Their father doesn't have long to live; the stroke has left him weak, and while the medics reckon that he might make it through to the summer, this is by no means certain.

The main purpose of the trip is relaxation, but he knows that his dad needs to see Uncle Rodney before he dies. After the stroke, Rodney was the only word he could say. Everything was Rodney: the dog, a cup of tea, Tony fucking Blair – they were all Rodney. Speech therapy has helped his dad regain some of his vocabulary, but the name Rodney keeps coming up again and again, and the consensus among the family is that it would be good to track down their long-absent uncle.

David has used his inheritance well. He invested in a series of buy-to-let mortgages, turning his three hundred thousand into a steady and lucrative income stream. Like his uncle Rodney, he's never really had a job. He has a bachelor's degree and is pretty streetwise, but he never much liked working as an end in itself, and his property portfolio gives him the freedom not to do very much. His life has consisted of bringing in rent, shagging around, playing a guitar in a band and taking drugs.

He's footloose, tending to see a long-term relationship as

being something that lasts more than two weekends, and he has loads of mates to hang around with. He's funny, popular, cheeky and a bit of a maverick, and forever getting into fights. People used to joke that he could start one in an empty room, but in reality he's just a bit fearless. He knows how to handle himself, and he doesn't suffer fools gladly. Most of the time he comes off the better, and on occasions where he doesn't, he knows enough people who'll give a scumbag a good hiding on his behalf.

If asked, he explains that he's a company director. This makes him giggle inside, but it's also true. His company, Cathy Kellison Property Holdings (CKPH), is named after the mum he hardly knew, largely because he calculated, correctly, that people would be less aggressive towards a business that carried a woman's name. Trade is good, and he's about to diversify into other areas, and in particular online porn sites. He's heard that the business is easy, as most of the source material comes from the States and Eastern Europe. All he'd have to do is host it, sell advertising space and watch the cash roll in.

His ambition one day is to own Tranmere Rovers, but to do that he needs an annual turnover in excess of £5 million. He'd pay himself a 20 per cent dividend and set aside a further 10 per cent for a small team of assistants; the rest would be invested back into the club. He's good at two things above all else: making money and making friends, and he reckons that these attributes will enable him to succeed where so many fail in the world of professional football.

The trip to Australia is, ostensibly, a business expense. Gordon Brown, the Chancellor, is paying for him to explore the potential for CKPH to invest in property abroad, and the way David sees it, the more he denies the British government in tax, the less money they'll have to bomb the shit out of innocent people in Iraq and elsewhere. He firmly believes that wasting money on foreign wars to protect America's oil interest is a con and that the same money could be going into the creaking National Health Service. He's inherited his father's politics, if not his principles, so as far as he's concerned, every bastard is on the rob, so fuck 'em!

Like his uncle Rodney, David is also a bit of a loner. It isn't that he's antisocial, far from it – he's never happier than when he's in a club knocking back the shots and buying rounds for his mates – but he's a loner in the sense that he doesn't *need* other people around him for company. In this respect, Australia is perfect, as he can mingle, mix, make his own decisions and chat women up to his heart's content.

His solo quest to find Rodney is proving to be impossible, but that's not to say it hasn't been enjoyable. He's found a number of bars that show live English football, and so drinking beer at 1a.m. while watching lunchtime games, or at 6a.m. for evening kick-offs, has been an unexpected novelty. He quickly realised that only the dregs of society are still up for the 6a.m. games, though, and he's pretty sure that Rodney doesn't fit that description. The 1a.m. games are better attended, but even then, most of the punters were pissed as farts and more interested in drinking than watching football. Again, he isn't sure if Rodney fits this profile.

One day, he's sitting outside a cafe in Darlinghurst, drinking excellent coffee and wearing a Rovers shirt, when a woman walks past and does a double take.

'My God,' she says, pointing at the badge on his chest, 'is that a Tranmere shirt?'

Her accent is Australian, but there's a vague hint of a northern English there, too.

'Dead right,' he says, playing it cool. 'Not too many people know who Tranmere are around here.'

'My ex-husband supported them,' the woman explains.

Looking closely at her, it seems to David that she's younger than the age he imagines Laura to be, but this is too good an opportunity to miss.

'Wow, it's kind of mad to meet a woman who even knows who Tranmere are out here,' he says, 'never mind one who was married to a Rovers supporter. Can I buy you a coffee?'

Play it cool, he keeps telling himself. *Play it cool*.

The woman glances around, looking unsure for a second.

'Alright, then,' she says, seemingly relaxing. 'I'm in no hurry, so why not.'

'So,' he asks once she's sat down and a barista has taken her order, 'you from Birkenhead?'

'No,' she says, 'I grew up in Liverpool. My husband was from Birkenhead, though.'

'Oh, right. So, how long you been here for?'

'Oh, donkey's years, love. It's been over thirty years now.'

'You came here when you were only nineteen, then?'

'You're a bit of a player, aren't you?' she laughs. 'God, I do miss that Scouse cheekiness.'

'Don't know what you mean, love.' He holds his hands up in mock defence. 'I mean, you can't be more than late forties.'

'Quite a bit more,' she smiles.

While the woman is pleasant, she's also guarded and doesn't give much away. He decides to press her a bit harder.

'So, how come you got divorced?'

'God,' she exclaims, 'what do you do for a living, are you a cop?'

It's now David's turn to laugh.

'I run my own company,' he says. 'Property development, mostly rentals.'

'Oh, good for you. Is that here in Sydney?'

'No, the business is back in Liverpool. I'm just evaluating the potential of the rental market here.'

Their conversation continues, with the woman wanting to

know how Liverpool has changed. David tells her that there's no longer a Dockers' Umbrella but that despite being destroyed in the eighties, the city is now on the up, with its imminent European Capital of Culture status having a transformative effect.

'Don't you ever go back?' he asks.

'Never. There's nothing there for me now. All my friends and distractions are here in Sydney.'

He knows that he has to get a name.

'I'm here for another ten days before heading back. Could I buy you dinner one evening? I've yet to try Doyles, on the bay.'

'Fish and chips?' she laughs.

'It's supposed to be good, isn't it?'

'Yeah, yeah, it's fine. It's just a bit ironic that you've come all this way and want fish and chips.'

'How about tomorrow evening?'

'Yeah, go on, then.'

'I'm David, by the way.'

'I'm Laura.'

His heart skips a beat, but he doesn't dare show it on his face. *Play it cool!*

'Eight o'clock?' he suggests.

'Great, I'll meet you there,' she smiles.

He waves goodbye as she disappears around a corner at the end of the street, and then he immediately looks for an internet cafe to email his brother from.

From: Tranmere-boy-down-under
To: BJ Kellison
Date: 16 February 2005

Bazza!

A breakthrough, by pure chance.

I've just met this woman who recognised my Tranmere shirt. She's the right age and her name is… Laura! She was formerly married to a Tranmere supporter and is now divorced. She also left Liverpool at exactly the right time to be the right Laura.

I'm having dinner with her tomorrow night, a place called Doyles on the Beach.

I think I'm a genius. I have, I'm 100 per cent sure, found her.

More after dinner tomorrow.

David

That night, his sleep is fitful. He tosses and turns, waking several times and jotting down questions to ask her as he tries to work out how to gain the maximum amount of information without showing his hand. He also needs to make sure that she doesn't work out who he is.

After a bit more thought, he wonders if it would be easier simply to answer her questions truthfully, but only if she asks them. He has no reason to lie to her and nothing to hide, but then, on the other hand, he has no idea how she and Rodney ended up in Australia. *Why did they leave?* he thinks. *What happened that meant they could never return? What's her relationship to Dad? Were they friends or actually lovers? What if she's not the Laura I'm looking for? Surely, there can't be two of them in Sydney who are the same age and both from Liverpool, and who both married a Tranmere supporter, can there?*

By morning, he's exhausted. He stays in bed right through until lunchtime, and it's only when room service knocks at his door that he properly wakes.

Today is the day.

He waits at a table in Doyles for more than an hour, until

eventually that Kellison sense of optimism begins to fade. She isn't coming. He's been duped.

*

That morning, before she was due to meet David at Doyles, Laura decided to catch up with Rodney. They hadn't talked in a while, and she felt inspired to give him a call.

'Hiya, Rodney,' she said. 'I'm having dinner with a Rovers supporter tonight!'

'Are we supposed to be meeting up?' Rodney asked, a slight panic in his voice.

Laura was one for commemorating anniversaries, and he was obviously worried that another significant milestone, of which there were many, was upon them. There was the first time they met, their dry run at Littlewoods, their stay at The Ritz, their arrival in Oz, moving into their first apartment… the list was endless. It was an exaggeration to say that they had three hundred and sixty-five anniversaries a year, but it often felt like that was the case.

'Not you!' she giggled.

'You know another Rovers supporter?' He sounded sceptical. 'In Sydney?'

'A young man I met on Darlinghurst Road yesterday.'

Rodney went quiet for a moment and then asked, 'How old was he?'

'I dunno, but there's no need for you to get all possessive on me. I'm old enough to be his nan.'

'That's what bothers me.'

He then explained that he'd heard rumours about a guy visiting sports bars in Sydney, trying to find a Tranmere fan named Rodney.

'You're being paranoid,' she laughed.

149

'Maybe, but maybe not. How old did you say this guy was?'

'I guess early-thirties, or mid-thirties at most.'

'There you go. That's exactly what people said about the bloke who's been asking after me.'

'Nah, it's just a coincidence.'

Rodney had never believed in coincidences. In his experience, they didn't really exist. Things happened for a reason, not because random acts drew people together by chance. He'd say that it wasn't a coincidence when Abraham Lincoln bumped into an assassin at the theatre, just like it wasn't a coincidence that Princess Diana's car was being pursued by the paparazzi. To him, coincidence was just another word for superstition.

'You're wrong,' he said as the conversation started to turn into the kind of toxic exchanges that couples have at the end of their relationships, after common ground has given way to mutual contempt.

'You're being daft,' Laura said.

'No, you're being dead soppy,' he countered. 'What was this guy's name?'

'David.'

Rodney took a sharp breath.

'David what?'

'I don't know! I didn't ask him.'

'I bet it was Kellison!'

'Rodney, you really are daft,' she sighed. 'I was ringing for a chat, and now you're interrogating me about some random stranger, on a planet filled with billions of people, being your relative. I'm putting the phone down.'

She hung up, but the doubts had been sown in her mind. She hadn't known that someone had been looking for Rodney. It could be a cop, or one of Reggie's kids looking for more money. Neither she nor Rodney had ever overcome their status as fugitives, despite them knowing that no questions had ever been asked about the pools win.

She wondered what to do. The simplest thing would be not to turn up, but that wouldn't resolve anything. After thinking it through, she decided that she'd get there early, take a corner table and, with a bit of luck, slip out unnoticed once she'd snapped a photo of him on her phone. She knew some of the waiters at Doyles, and that she'd be able to rely on them to be discreet. With David being a tourist, chances were that he'd choose an outside table, which would give her the opportunity to take a few pictures to send on to Rodney.

As she studies the pictures, Laura concedes that the eyes are definitely like Reggie's. The physique, too; rounded shoulders but with a broad chest. David's better-looking than Reggie, like an updated version of the same car, but you can still tell that they're from the same factory.

Rodney calls twenty minutes later.

'I reckon that's defo our David,' he says. 'Did you talk to him?'

'No,' she says, 'not after you spooked me. I took the pictures after he sat down.'

'Good.'

'I wonder what he's after. Money, maybe?'

'Possibly, but I don't think money's a problem. Reggie put everything he got into a trust fund, and each of his kids got paid out when they turned twenty-one.'

'That makes sense, actually. He said he was a company director, and I certainly didn't get the impression that he was skint.'

'*And* he supports Tranmere,' Rodney says, suddenly sounding full of pride.

'I've already told you that!'

'Is Reggie with him?'

'No, he said he's travelling alone.'

*

Rodney is both relieved and disappointed after his conversation with Laura. He's always hoped that he might see Reggie again one day, but it was the very faintest of hopes, like hoping Tranmere won the Champions League, or that England would win the World Cup again. He's left with the thought that it might have been better if Laura had met David. That way, he'd at least have got to see his nephew and could have caught up on all the family news. If David's after money, he'll get a short shrift, but if, on the other hand, he's just making a social visit, then that's a different matter.

Rodney begins to imagine having a beer with the David formerly known as Baby; talking about life back in Birkenhead and discussing Tranmere's prospects.

*

From: Tranmere-boy-down-under

To: BJ Kellison

Date: 17 February 2005

Bazza,

She didn't fucking turn up! Waited for an hour, and then had a meal on my own.

Had a few beers on the way back to the hotel – bit pissed now. Really annoyed!

David

From: BJ Kellison
To: Tranmere-boy-down-under
Date: 18 February 2005

David,

That's very disappointing. You were so close by the sound of it.

Stay calm. You've done your best, mate.

Barry

*

Judging by the fact that Laura met him on Darlinghurst Road, Rodney reckons that David's probably staying in one of the mid-priced hotels in that area. After making a few notes, he starts making calls, determined to capitalise on Australia's famed commitment to providing great customer service.

'Hi there,' he says, reading from his script. 'I've got my nephew visiting Sydney, but the thing is, he said he was staying around your area, but I've only gone and lost his mobile number! David Kellison's his name – British guy, Liverpool accent. Is he staying with you, by any chance?'

A couple of the hotels refuse to give out their guests' details but do at least confirm that they have nobody of that description staying with them. On something like the sixth attempt, he gets lucky.

'Ah, yeah,' the guy on the end of the phone says, 'he's just gone out. Do you want to leave a message?'

'No, no, it's OK,' Rodney says, 'I'll try him again later. Can you not mention I called? I want to surprise him.' He adds a conspiratorial laugh.

'Sure,' the guy laughs along. 'He's usually around late afternoon, if you want to try to catch him then.'

'Thanks, mate, that's smashing!' Rodney beams and then hangs up.

The hotel, Spicers Potts Point, is slightly more upmarket than those he'd tried first – a boutique-type affair, about five minutes' walk from Darlinghurst Road, and easy enough to get to.

Rodney wonders what to do next. He doesn't want to risk introducing himself to David, as that would be too risky; he needs to be wary, at least to begin with. He decides, therefore, to put on an old Everton shirt he was once gifted and sit himself in a bar across the way from the hotel. If David's wearing his Tranmere gear again, the odds of two Scousers meeting in Sydney will be grounds for starting a conversation.

The first couple of attempts he makes are unsuccessful, but then it becomes a case of third time lucky, as David walks past just as Rodney's ordering himself another schooner.

'Is that a Tranmere shirt, mate?' Rodney calls out.

David stops and looks around, and he then grins when he notices the Everton shirt.

'Fucking hell,' he cries, 'an Evertonian! You're probably still smartin' about us dumping you out of the FA Cup back in 2001!'

'You were lucky that day,' Rodney says.

'Fuck off, we were lucky. We played you off the park! Half Gwladys Street disappeared when we went two up. I mean, Christ, it's Tranmere. We need a ten-goal head start, and even then we usually fuck it up!'

'Can I buy you a beer?'

'Normally, I'd walk a million miles from an Evertonian offering to buy me a drink, but it's a warm evening and I'm in the mood for a chat.'

'Good man,' Rodney laughs as David joins him at the table. 'I'm Fred, by the way.'

'What're you doing out here, Fred?' David asks.

'I live here – have done for years,' Rodney says, reminding himself not to mention exactly how many years. 'What about you? You here on holiday?'

'Sort of,' David sighs. 'I'm also meant to be here on business, but I'm really here on a mercy mission.'

'Sounds interesting.'

'Frustrating, more like. I've been trying to track down this uncle of mine, who's also a Tranmere supporter and is apparently living somewhere in these parts. I even managed to track down a woman who I was convinced was his ex-wife – was meant to have dinner with her and everything, but then she never showed up. Fucking annoying!'

'I don't think I've never come across a Tranmere supporter down here.'

'Plenty of Liverpool fans, though. They're ten a penny in Sydney.'

'I hate the Red Shite. Bunch of fucking telly clappers, most of them. Tunnel rats, too.'

'Well, I'll tell you, most kids who support them here only do so because they want a successful English team to follow. Don't think I've met another Evertonian out here on the streets, like.'

'Why did you say you were here, then?'

'I never did, did I?' David said. He continued, 'It's me dad. He's really ill, and I want to contact me uncle Rodney because it seems like Dad wants to see him before he passes.'

Rodney feels himself getting a little choked at the news that Reggie's ill.

'Your dad got cancer or something?' he asks.

'No, no, nothing like that. He had a stroke, and now he keeps having these mini-strokes. At first, they only happened once every three months or so, but now they're happening every couple of weeks. The quacks reckon it's only a matter of time before one of them kills him.'

'That sounds terrible,' Rodney says, genuinely moved. 'It's hard to imagine Reggie being in a state like that.'

'Say that again, *Fred*?' David says, looking Rodney straight in the eye while emphasising his fake name.

'I'm just saying, it must be tough.' Rodney forces a cough, realising his error.

'But you didn't say that, did you? You said Reggie, and I haven't even told you his name, have I?' David stands and starts jabbing his finger into Rodney's chest. 'Who the fucking hell are you, eh? You shitty, no-mark, blue-nose scum!'

'Alright, calm down, kid.'

'I won't fucking calm down until you tell me who the fuck you are! How come you fucking know me dad's name when I never said it?'

Just when it looked as though his nephew was about to lay one on him, Rodney watched as the lad's brain suddenly clicked into gear.

'It's you, isn't it?' David says. 'You're fucking Rodney!'

'He's a smashing lad,' Rodney says as he drops onto Laura's couch and stretches out. 'Foul temper, like, and a foul mouth to go with it, but he's decent.'

Laura looks at him sceptically.

'I can't keep up with you. One minute you want nothing to do with him, and the next you're hunting him down for a beer!'

Rodney looks sheepish.

'He's blood,' he explains with a shrug.

'And what about Reggie?' she asks, softening her tone.

'Well, like I say, it sounds like he's in a very bad way.'

Poor Reggie, she thinks, nodding sympathetically, *a long-*

time widower, and now not far from death's door himself. His life hasn't been the happiest, and she's sad to learn that the end is close. Would things have been different if she'd stuck to their original plan, or are some people just fated to lead unfulfilling lives?

'Are you going to go back?'

He takes a deep breath and blows his cheeks out.

'Well, I...' he starts but then gets a bit teary and pauses.

She moves closer to him and takes his hand in hers.

'I kind of want to,' he tries again, barely managing to keep his emotions in check. 'The thing is, though, I'm not really sure what difference me going would make at this point.'

'It might make a difference to Reggie,' she says gently.

'Will you come, too?'

She's been dreading this inevitable question, and she already has her answer.

'From what David has said, I don't think that would be a good idea. Seeing me might cause him a lot of emotional pain. It might even tip him over the edge.'

Rodney nods. It isn't the answer he wants to hear, but then she's good like that. She tells things as they are and not how you want to hear them.

'Does me not wanting to come affect your decision?' she asks.

'No, to be honest. I never really thought you would. I'm going to sleep on it. There's a part of me that wants to let sleeping dogs lie, and another that wants to see him again before he goes.'

Laura nods. She understands.

'Whatever happens,' he continues, 'I've at least made contact with David. That's a good thing.'

He hasn't lost his knack for turning negatives into positives, she smiles, and then she kisses him on the cheek before looking into his eyes and giving him a huge smile. 'You're *so* soppy sometimes, Rodney,' she says, and they share a laugh.

*

From: Tranmere-boy-down-under
To: BJ Kellison
Date: 22 February 2005

Bazza,

I've tracked him down, although there was a point where I might have struck him down!

We spent most of yesterday evening talking. He seems interested in possibly coming back, but he isn't 100 per cent sure. I tried to persuade him, but he's like Mum was – a bit stubborn at times.

He seems quite likeable. He's made his money from retail investments out here – doing very well for himself. I'm going to meet Laura and him for lunch tomorrow. He said they'll let me know if both, one or neither of them will be making the journey.

Fingers crossed, big fella!

David

From: BJ Kellison
To: Tranmere-boy-down-under
Date: 23 February 2005

Hi David,

Well done for finding him.

Not sure if it's a good idea for both of them to come. I suspect that seeing Laura would cause Dad quite a lot of distress.

I'll wait for you to get home to tell me the full story about how this came about. Everything can wait.

In regard to Dad, his position is described as 'stable'. He's no worse, no better. It's the 'no better' bit that's worrying.

Take care,

Barry

*

It's a warm day – probably one of the warmest David's experienced since arriving in Australia – and by late morning, the temperature is up in the high twenties. It's scheduled to get as high as thirty-four degrees by mid-afternoon, when he's arranged to meet Rodney and Laura at The Rocks. There's a bar there that Rodney likes, which does 'simple' food and good beer; nothing too fancy.

By the time David arrives, Laura and Rodney are already seated on the roof terrace, from which you can watch the ferries make their way across the bay to their various destinations. It's like looking at a boating lake or a model village.

There's a beer waiting for David when he reaches the table, and to begin with they make idle small talk. However, this soon gives way to the most pressing item on the agenda.

'Have you made your mind up, then?' David asks Rodney.

'I think so, yeah,' he replies.

'What about you, Laura?'

'Yep,' she says with a firm nod.

'Go on, then.'

'Well, listen, it's like this…' She removes the oversized sunglasses that she's been hiding behind. 'I was very fond of your dad, David, but I think he had even stronger feelings for me. So, the way I see it is that if I go, I'll simply cause him even more distress. That won't be good, you know. I don't wanna make him any worse than he already is.'

'I'm not here to stick my nose into anyone's past,' David says. 'I've no idea what went on between the three of you, and I reckon that you're best placed to judge what you should do for yourselves.' He turns to Rodney. 'What about you, Unc?'

This brings a smile to Rodney's face, but it quickly disappears as he remembers the seriousness of the matter at hand.

'If I'm really honest, I don't want to go back to Merseyside. You know, I've thought about it a lot – hardly slept last night because of it.'

David's disappointed, but he allows his uncle to continue.

'The thing is…' Rodney takes a large gulp of beer and sighs deeply. 'The thing is, you're the nearest I have to family, along with your dad, and I can't simply ignore that.'

'Right, I don't understand this.' David gets agitated, almost aggressive. 'Are you saying that you're not coming, either?'

Laura places a hand on David's arm, but he shrugs it off.

'Listen,' Rodney says, 'just calm down, eh?'

'Well, you stop talking like fucking Yoda, then!' David shouts.

Rodney takes another deep breath.

'David, I've made up my mind. I might regret it, but I'm not somebody who likes to live with regrets. So, I've decided I'm going to see Reggie.'

David has to do a double take.

'You mean you're coming?'

'That's what I said, isn't it?'

Then hard, angry little David stands up and gestures for Rodney to do the same. He wraps his arms around him in a huge, life-affirming hug.

'Thank you for this,' David says quietly, 'thank you. Dad'll be made up.'

On a late-summer's afternoon, halfway across the world, Rodney has agreed to return to his roots. Only time will tell if this is the decision of a wise man, or that of a fool.

The Hilbre Court nursing home in West Kirby isn't the Ritz. For a start, too often its corridors smell of overcooked cabbage and disinfectant for it to be viewed in the same light as its London counterpart. While it's true that at The Ritz, the average age of residents isn't far off that of Hilbre Court, there the comparisons end. Hilbre Court isn't somewhere you go to party; it's the place you go to die.

In Room 27, Reggie Kellison lies in his bed. It's three o'clock on a late-February afternoon, and all things considered, he isn't feeling too bad. His mobility is very poor, and worse still, his speech is mostly incomprehensible. Whenever he tries to express himself, saying for example, 'The food in this place is crap,' all that comes out is, 'The Rodney, Rodney here, crap Rodney.' This tends to confuse people, not least Reggie himself. He thinks that what he's saying makes perfect sense, and he has no inkling that his communication is about as easy to understand as a party political broadcast by the Tories.

Speech therapy is helping, though. A few weeks ago, he was only managing one loud, continuous groan that came out as 'R-od-en-ee.' Now, at least, he's able to add 'and', 'if' and 'the' to his sentences. This is progress. The speech therapists and other staff all looked really pleased as he managed to utter these extra sounds. He's also had another breakthrough this week, which his therapist is very excited about. Even though the effort leaves him feeling like he's run a marathon, he can now say, 'How now brown cow.' It comes out slowly, like a 33rpm record being played at 16rpm, but it's comprehensible.

Walking is also difficult, as the multiple strokes have left him unable to move at anything more than a snail's pace, and even that requires support from a three-pronged silver walking stick. This gives him the stability that his body's no longer capable of on its own, but the stick is heavy and slows him down even further. Unlike with his dysphasia, Reggie is aware of his reduced mobility, and it greatly distresses him.

His closest and longest-standing friend, Fred, appears next to the bed. Unlike Reggie, Fred's enjoying extremely good health in his old age. He drinks far less now, and the results are there for all to see.

'Right then, Reggie,' he says cheerfully, 'I've brought tonight's *Echo*, this morning's *Daily Mirror* and the *Wirral Globe*, although the last one is a load of crap, if you ask me.'

Fred laughs, and Reggie manages a weak smile. Laughing is still beyond him at this point.

'It's Friday, so the only place to start is on the back page,' Fred says.

He then carefully reads through the football section, starting with Tranmere and then going on to Liverpool, followed by a final mention of Everton.

Even though he isn't much of a football fan, he does his best to comment on what he's reading, adding things like, 'I think Stevie G's getting a bit of unfair criticism there, don't you?' Or, 'If I were Everton, I'd never have touched Gascoigne with a barge pole! He's a gobshite, that one. They've never made a decent signing since!'

Reggie really appreciates his mate's efforts. At a time when the majority of his daily interactions are with nurses or ancillary staff, Fred keeps him tethered to normality. After he finishes with the *Echo*, he starts on the *Mirror* but then remembers that he has news to pass on.

'Oh, by the way, I got a call from your Barry. Guess what?'

Asking a dysphasic man a question like that is a bit like asking someone dying of thirst if he prefers red or white wine, but Reggie manages to shrug his shoulders with what he hopes is a degree of enthusiasm.

'Well,' Fred says, 'it seems that your David has been in Sydney, you know, in Australia?'

Reggie nods, despite having no earthly idea why Fred feels the need to remind him of this. David came to see him a few weeks ago, before he left.

'So, guess who he met out there?' At this, Fred's eyes become wide, like a little boy telling his friend a secret. 'Your Rodney!' he announces triumphantly.

Reggie's response is something along the lines of, 'Rodney, Rodney, fuck, Rodney-bastard-Rodney!'

'You what?' Fred chuckles.

Reggie repeats himself, and Fred just laughs. This makes Reggie even more annoyed, as what he's trying to say is, 'Why on God's earth would I fucking want to see that prat?'

'He'll be here in a few days,' Fred says enthusiastically.

Reggie lets out a deep sigh. *Is my condition really that bad?* he wonders. *Has the time come for all manner of people who I don't want to see to come and pay their last respects at my bedside? Surely not.*

Reggie tries to wave his left arm dismissively.

'What, have you had enough now?' Fred asks.

Reggie nods affirmatively. He's had enough of lying in a hospital bed, and of people not understanding what he's saying. He really is exhausted by everything around him.

Fred gathers his things together.

'I'll pop in for a bit tomorrow with the *Football Echo*, mate,' he says on his way out.

Reggie's left alone again, annoyed and frustrated. He wants to know why the fuck the family has decided that Rodney should visit him.

PART 4

'Stumbling is not falling'
                        Malcolm X

MORE
RECENT TIMES

When Rodney gets back to Sydney, he immediately feels like he needs to go to Melbourne and reconnect with his male friends. Being back in Merseyside for six weeks has left him feeling oppressed, depressed and perplexed.

It hadn't been the journey he'd expected, for so many different reasons. He thought he was going to be feted as the returning hero, but instead it felt like there were times that he was treated like a pariah. He just didn't fit in back where he grew up, and where he grew up didn't make any effort to accommodate him. It was strange. He'd expected to be made welcome, but at times he was simply shunned, or at best seen as being irrelevant, like a Christmas fairy discovered under the sofa at Easter.

Of course, there were some positives. He made two trips to Prenton Park and was amazed as to how the ground had been transformed. No longer a rickety, creaking stadium, it was now a modern sports venue. He went slightly mad in the club shop, largely because he knew he was never going to return to England, at least not in the short-term, anyway.

He went out with David a couple of times and with Barry once. He likes how his relationship with David has grown stronger and stronger, and that his youngest nephew doesn't seem to judge him. Barry hadn't changed much from when he'd last seen him. A confident but gentle guy, he's now married with a couple of kids, and living well down in Dorset. *On reflection*, he thinks, *that might have made the trip worthwhile in its own right.*

Other aspects of the journey hadn't gone so well, though.

Reggie's still alive and, if anything, he seemed to be getting stronger. There had been some progress with his speech, although he still wasn't putting coherent sentences together. In part, this was because shortly after Rodney arrived, he'd stopped repeating his name, and instead utilised a lexicon of swear words that would make a trooper blush.

Upon entering Reggie's room at the nursing home, Rodney had been greeted with, 'Cunt, prick, twat, Rodney.'

Other members of the family would try to interpret what Reggie was saying. On this occasion, Kay was in the room.

She was holding Reggie's hand and said, 'I think he said he's really pleased to see you, Rodney.'

Yet, Reggie's face suggested that he was far from pleased. His eyes glared with an anger that Rodney recognised from the distant past, and it was also noticeable that when someone like Fred or David was in the room, his tone was much gentler. So, for example, he would greet David with, 'David, arse, son, tit-wank, OK?'

If anybody had been able to translate what Reggie was saying, they'd have realised that his greeting for Rodney was actually, 'Cunt, prick, twat, Rodney,' but no one really paid much attention. Reggie was dysphasic, so trying to understand him was viewed as a mug's game.

Added to this, whenever Rodney was alone with Reggie, the man in the bed would look away or decide to sleep. Their bond didn't really grow stronger. If anything, it became more strained.

During the second week of his stay, he was having tea with Lynn, who'd taken the afternoon off work because she wanted to catch up with her long-absent uncle. She'd explained that Cathy had left a note for him, with the instruction that it was to be destroyed it if he never came back to England.

'Right,' he said, 'so where is it, then?'

'Well, this is the thing,' Lynn said, 'I've lost it. But I'm doing my best to find it, so that you can have it before you go back.'

This left Rodney even more perplexed. It was as if nobody really acknowledged his position in the family. Laura had also sent a letter for Reggie, which he expected that he'd be able to read to him, but when he made the offer to do this, Reggie indicated that he wanted David to read it to him.

'David, no Rodney, twat, arsehole,' was the response as he shook his head vehemently.

All of this had left Rodney feeling bewildered and disorientated. He'd made a positive gesture by returning to Merseyside to see his brother-in-law, who was, allegedly, calling for him on his deathbed. Yet, the feeling he got was that he was about as welcome as a hunt saboteur at the annual hunt dinner.

It's a wet April afternoon, and David's sitting down to read the letter from Laura to his father.

'Are you sure about this, Dad?' he asks.

'Penis?' Reggie says.

'Do you want me to read this to you?'

'Yes, cocksucker.'

David laughs loudly and smiles.

'That phrase might be better used on Uncle Rodney, don't you think?' He tilts his head to one side.

Reggie smiles, too, but he's frustrated that he can't make himself understood.

'Right,' David says, 'I'll read it dead slowly. If you want me to go back and read a bit again, or, well, you know, just touch my arm, OK?'

Reggie nods, grateful for the effort that his son is making. He knows that David's a bit of a wild one, but also that he's a good kid at heart.

'Here goes.'

David clears his throat and begins:

Dearest Reggie,

I was so sorry to hear the news about your stroke. I remember you as a proud, kind man, and I know that strokes often leave people in a strange place, lacking dignity or the ability to communicate. I suspect you'll be as distressed as the rest of your family are by your current situation, but I know that you'll be doing your best to recover.

David looks up. There's a tear in Reggie's eye.

'Clitoris,' the old man says gently.

'Shall I carry on?' David asks.

'Arse.' Reggie nods.

Writing to you after all these years is a strange and difficult experience. Sometimes it feels like no time has passed since we were last together. We had a great deal to thank Aunty Eileen for, didn't we?

Reggie smiles at this and nods for David to continue.

I know that you'll be disappointed that things didn't work out as we planned. I think Rodney's already explained that I couldn't have it on my conscience, being a not-particularly-good Catholic girl, to be responsible for breaking up your marriage and your family.

David glances at his father. He's clearly uncomfortable with some of this stuff, but he soldiers on.

Despite this, hardly a day has gone by without me thinking about you. I've carried a different kind of guilt; the guilt of not fulfilling a promise. This is, I've discovered, just as hard to bear. I suspect that you won't believe this, but all I can say is it's the honest truth. I never wanted to hurt you, never wanted to upset you, and I never betrayed you to Rodney.

I want you to get better. I want you to concentrate every fibre of your being on getting better, because I know that the Reggie Kellison I knew wouldn't let this set him back too far.

Reggie's now crying.
'Are you sure you want me to continue?' David asks again.
'Tit wank.' Reggie nods.

I met David while he was here in Sydney. He's a lovely man. Reminds me a bit of you. You obviously brainwashed him into following Tranmere, but aside from that he seems quite decent. I explained to him that I didn't think it was a good idea for me to come with Rodney. My feeling is that this would have upset you too much, but if I'm honest, Reggie, I was too much of a coward to make the journey.

I didn't want to come home to see you in a bed, immobile and unable to communicate properly. That's not the Reggie I want to have a memory of. The Reggie I want to remember was the funny, polite and sincere man from all those years ago, who I fell in love with but then ran away from.

I know that I caused you pain, and I hope you can forgive me. For my part, there will always be a piece of my heart with your name engraved on it, and that will be the case until my dying day.

Be strong, Reggie. Get well and use the love in this letter as a potion to aid your recovery.

With love and kisses from the other side of the world,

Laura.

Rainfall rattles against the windows, but between father and son there's only silence. For a while, David stares down at the floor before finally looking up at his dad.

'Do you want me to read it again?' he asks.

Reggie shakes his head, and then, for the first time in almost a year, he's able to express himself, if not clearly then at least in staccato.

He looks David in the eye and says the words, 'Burn... secret,' and then puts one trembling finger to his lips.

David understands.

'Back in five minutes,' he says, and then he kisses his father on the forehead and leaves the room.

In the Hilbre Court car park, David takes a lighter out of his pocket and sets fire to Laura's letter before dropping the pages into a nearby empty rubbish bin. As he watches the pages burn, he thinks about what he's just read. There are lots of questions to ask, but none that he needs to know the answer to. This is something that lives in the past, not the present. In his mind nothing can change what has happened. All anyone can do is try to make tomorrow a better day.

He goes back inside to find his father lying still with his eyes closed, and for a terrible moment, he thinks that he may have passed away, content to have received Laura's love, safe in the knowledge that she still cared about him. He ran to the bed and shook his dad's shoulders.

'Fuck!' Reggie shouts, jolted from his peaceful slumber.

'Sorry, Dad,' David laughs. 'I was scared that you'd gone then!'

Reggie smiled. 'Cocksucker,' he says softly and closes his eyes.

*

About a week before the end of his visit home, Rodney was joined by Lynn and David for a drink at a pub in West Kirby. The White Horse was a place that he'd frequented many years before, and he was happy to see that it hadn't changed. He even thought that the bar staff looked like the same people who'd worked there back in the sixties, although obviously he knew that it wasn't actually them.

Lynn had been looking conspiratorial all evening, making furtive glances at him.

Eventually, she said, 'David, I think it's my round, but if I give you the money, would you go up and get them in?'

'I'm not your fuckin' maid,' David replied, slightly worse for the drink.

'Go on, love, please,' she said pleadingly.

He reluctantly took a ten-pound note from her and huffed his way towards the bar, and as soon as he was gone, she hissed to Rodney, 'I found it!'

'What?' Rodney asked, also fairly inebriated.

'The letter,' she said. 'The letter from my mum.'

'Can I have it, then?'

'Don't be daft, not in here!'

Rodney sighed, wondering why she was so intent on turning this into her own personal little drama.

'You two hatching something?' David asked, returning from the bar.

Lynn laughed mockingly. 'You're so paranoid, David.'

'We were just talking about the olden days, before you were born,' Rodney said.

David looked unconvinced, but he also seemed to be at the stage where he was more interested in the beer than anything else. As he stared into his glass, perhaps contemplating the flavour and taste to come, Lynn looked to Rodney and mouthed, 'Later.'

Rodney was getting pretty frustrated with his niece by this point. He just wanted a quiet evening in the pub, chatting about nothing in particular. It's why he liked hanging around with David, who could do footy, politics or general gossip. Lynn was more like a frantic nun, always wanting something spectacular to happen.

'I'll drop you at the Green Lodge,' David said to Rodney as they finished their drinks.

'You can't take him back,' Lynn protested. 'You're in no fit state to drive.'

'I'll be fine,' David insisted.

'No, leave your car here, David,' Rodney said.

About ten minutes later, having dropped David at his flat, Lynn fished around in her handbag, which seemed to be cavernous, until she eventually handed Rodney an envelope. It was marked with the words: *For Rodney's eyes only!*

'I don't know what's in it,' she said in what seemed a superfluous statement.

Back in his hotel room, Rodney poured himself a glass of whisky before opening the letter from his sister.

Dear Rodney,

If you're reading this, two things have happened. First, I've killed myself, and secondly, you're back in the UK.

I discovered, through your letters to Reggie, that he was having some sort of affair with Laura. You seem to have been part of this arrangement. You! My own brother, helping my husband to cavort with another woman!

I gave Reggie six kids and most of my life. I never interfered with his daft ideas, always saw him as a good man. He wasn't always the best father, but he wasn't the worst, either. Yet, when I found out about Laura, and how you seem to have known about it but not told me, everything went blank.

These are more words than you've probably ever heard me use, but I was content before. Do you know what that means, being content? It means you accept things for facts, and that you don't try to change them. Reggie wasn't Cary Grant, but then I wasn't Audrey Hepburn, so I suspect we were about right for each other.

Nothing matters now. Nothing. Everything feels like a big, empty lie, told to me by no-marks and fools. Even you, handsome Rodney. But you're not, are you? You're not the charming man who can get his way with any woman. No, you're a pervert who prefers men to women. That's just sick! Disgusting!

As for this Laura, whoever she is, she can burn in hell with you and Reggie. She can carry her sin to the grave, and then when she's judged – because we will all be judged, Rodney, make no mistake – she'll pay for it. The same for you and Reggie. Taking my own life is also a sin, but I'm banking it with the Holy Father against your accounts.

I'm your sister, so it's hard to sign this off without love and kisses, but then that would be false.

Rot in hell!

Cathy

Not for the first time since he arrived back in England, Rodney was left feeling punch-drunk. The vitriol in Cathy's letter shocked him. Worse still, the news that she'd killed herself chilled him to the marrow. *Does Reggie know?* he wondered. *Should I tell him?*

He knocked the whisky back in one go and poured himself another. Then, he sat and gathered his thoughts. The letter would need to remain a secret, he resolved. Barry had told him that the coroner had reached a verdict of death by misadventure, and now, all these years later, the letter could overcomplicate matters from the past. His distress and hurt at the tone of the words, and the accusation that he'd somehow been responsible for Reggie straying, was something else. *I took Laura away. I made sure that Reggie stayed with Cathy and the kids.*

That night, his whisky-fuelled dreams were fitful and disturbing. Images of their childhood together kept invading his head, except each happy scene of them playing together, or sharing a birthday party, was interrupted by Cathy screaming, *'Burn in hell!'* By the morning, he was more exhausted than he was when he went to bed. The following day was spent in a haze.

Late in the afternoon, he decided to go and see Reggie.

'Reggie,' Rodney said, nodding a solemn greeting to his brother-in-law.

Very slowly, Reggie managed to respond with, 'Hel-lo, Rodney.'

No swear words, no insults. Rodney was impressed.

'That's good, Reggie,' he said, giving him a thumbs up.

'Arse,' Reggie offered, like a First World War general ordering the heavy artillery to open fire again.

Rodney chose to ignore it.

'Reggie,' he went on, 'yesterday Lynn gave me a letter that had been written by Cathy before she died. It was very upsetting.'

Reggie tilted his head to one side inquisitively.

'There's stuff in there that I can't tell you about. She was obviously not in a good state of mind before she died.'

'Sad,' Reggie said with great effort.

'I don't think she was sad. She was furious with you, Laura and me.'

Reggie considered this information, and then, after weighing it up, he nodded.

'Your letters,' he said, and pointed to himself, 'me. Found.'

Reggie sighed, exhausted by the concentration required to make even this simple statement.

Rodney understood.

'It wasn't your fault,' he said.

Reggie nodded and then reached out his hand for Rodney to take. Reggie squeezed gently and nodded as a single tear rolled down his face.

Rodney looked down at the floor before finally raising his head and looking Reggie in the eye.

'We're okay, aren't we?'

Reggie nodded vigorously.

Rodney sighed deeply.

'I think I'll head back to Oz in the next few days.'

Reggie nodded again.

'There are things about this trip that have upset me. Things that I didn't want to look into but that I've had to.' Rodney paused, taking a big gulp of air. 'Despite that,' he said, struggling with his emotions, 'I'm really pleased I came. I've seen you, got to know David better and even seen Rovers, too!'

The mention of Rovers made them both laugh and broke the tension.

'You're getting stronger, you know, don't you?'

Reggie shrugged his shoulders.

'No, no, you are, Reggie. I can see it. I'm really pleased for you, okay?'

Reggie nodded.

'Right, I'd best be going.'

Reggie nodded.

'Up the Rovers, eh, Reggie,' Rodney turned and said as he reached the doorway. 'Up the Rovers!'

It was the last thing he ever said to his brother-in-law.

Reader, how do you know something's a mistake? Do you know it immediately, there and then, or do some mistakes require reflection? It might be that, over time, your decision to quit a job, buy a particular model of car or go on holiday to a certain place comes back to haunt you as an error of judgement. These are the worst kind of errors, are they not? The short-term ones, like treading in dog poo, leaving your wallet at home or taking the wrong junction on a motorway, well, they can be corrected almost straight away; the consequences are inconvenient but not devastating. Even if you don't wipe the dog poo off the sole of your shoe, the rain will eventually wash it away.

It's the big errors that come back to haunt us, such as voting the wrong way in a referendum, spending too much of your savings, or marrying the wrong person. Worse still, to admit to these errors makes us look like fools, lacking judgement or intelligence.

What would your advice to Rodney have been regarding the letter from Cathy? Hands up if it would be to leave it in the bottom of his suitcase? Yes, I thought a few of you might go for that one. How about burning the letter, like David did with Laura's missive? Hmm, not so many hands there. What about showing the letter to Laura? No hands. I'm with you on that, but sadly, tragically, Rodney is not.

*

After a few days in Melbourne, hanging out with the boys, all swagger and poise, while indulging his preferences, Rodney feels much better. He now wants to spend some time with Laura, as he needs to talk to her about what happened in England.

They meet for dinner at a Chinese restaurant, near to the Central Business District. It's a quiet June evening, right in the middle of winter, and a cold wind is blowing in off the harbour. Big coats and hats are required, with summer seeming more than a promise away.

Initially, their conversation isn't personal. They stick to benign topics, like how much everything had changed back home.

'I'll tell you,' Rodney says, 'the Albert Dock's amazing! There's a branch of the Tate there, too. All very sophisticated, not like the old Liverpool!'

Laura is wide-eyed, almost incredulous that Liverpool could be transformed like this.

'Oh, and Prenton Park!' Rodney beams. 'It's like bloody Wembley now!'

Laura laughs. She was enjoying Rodney's enthusiasm. It was the old Rodney that she'd first met. Funny, a bit outrageous, but always entertaining.

The conversation moves to Reggie.

'He's got stronger. His speech, to start with, well, it was just swear word after swear word,' Rodney laughs. 'God knows where he got it from. He was never a swearer, was he?'

Laura was enjoying all of this. Then Rodney changed his tone.

'There's something I need you to read,' he says.

'You written a book, Rodney?' she asks teasingly.

'Our Cathy wrote a letter to me before she...' He pauses, unsure if he should tell Laura that Cathy killed herself. He decides to be as vague as possible. 'Before she, erm, died.'

There is a moment's silence as the atmosphere becomes palpably sombre.

'I've got it here with me,' Rodney says. 'I want you to take it home and read it.'

'Can't I just read it now?' Laura asks.

'No, don't,' he says and hands it across the table to her. 'Take it home and read it later. We'll talk about it tomorrow.'

She reaches out and takes the letter, and gives him a funny grimace as she places it in her handbag. The mood soon lifts again, with Rodney returning to the lighter tone that they'd started the evening with.

Later that night, Laura reads Cathy's letter. As soon as she finishes, she immediately phones Rodney. She can't control the pain, and the tears are flowing freely.

'Why did you give that to me?' she asks, sobbing down the phone.

'Calm down, love,' Rodney replies, obviously taken aback by the emotion in her voice.

'Don't you see? Don't you realise how upsetting that is?

180

I'm *not* responsible for your sister's death, okay? Never in a million years! All that letter is is an outpouring of bile and jealousy. Did you just want to hurt me?'

'Laura, love, I'd never want to harm you,' he says gently. 'Surely you know that?'

'Then why in God's name did you give it to me, eh?'

'Do you want to come over to mine and talk face to face?'

'What good will that do? You gave me an unexploded bomb that's just gone off in my face!'

'That wasn't what I meant to do. I just wanted you to see what Cathy had written to me.'

'Why? What's your sister's nastiness got to do with me?'

'Well, she's blaming us, isn't she?'

'Rodney,' she says very firmly, 'do you think it's appropriate for anyone to take the blame when someone else takes their own life? Isn't it something that people look to do for a reason?'

Rodney goes quiet, and the only sound on the line is Laura crying.

'I'll come and see you tomorrow,' is all he can think to say before he hangs up.

For Laura, what follows is a restless night, where at times she feels as if morning will never come. Cathy's letter has rekindled her buried sense of Catholic guilt. Burning in hell, or worse yet, Purgatory, would be a terrible punishment for her. *Am I really responsible for Cathy's death?* she asks herself. *Should I accept at least some of the blame?* This, however, flies in the face of her own areligious logic. *Cathy chose to end her life. I can't be held accountable for that. It was her choice.*

However, the battle continues to rage within her. A sense of guilt, planted in her at an early age, the first time she heard about Original Sin, is winning the argument over and above candid logic.

When Rodney arrives at around 8a.m., she's still in bed. She answers the door in her dressing gown, but then goes straight back under the covers.

'Come on, Laura, love,' Rodney says from the doorway of her bedroom, 'this isn't like you.'

'I think we killed her,' she says quietly, almost whispering. 'Rodney, I'm sure that we have to accept some responsibility for this.'

He starts to get agitated.

'You're talking rubbish,' he says, raising his voice. 'This has bugger all to do with us, and everything to do with my sister.'

'You're wrong, Rodney. I think it's best that you should go now.'

She isn't cross or angry with him. She's just extremely saddened.

'I'm not going to leave you here,' he says. 'Look, get dressed, have a shower and let's go for breakfast, eh? We can go down to The Rocks.'

'I don't feel much like eating,' she replies flatly.

'Well, just keep me company, then,' he says, getting angry again.

She sits up and looks at him, marvelling at how detached he can be from his own sister's suicide. She swings her legs off the bed and points to the lounge area behind him.

'Go and wait through there while I get ready,' she says.

Not long later, they're eating breakfast in a cafe down at The Rocks.

Rodney gestures in the vague direction of a row of shops.

'Remember our fifth wedding anniversary?' he says, laughing.

'The tattoos?' she asks.

'Yeah, I mean, me getting a Tranmere crest was one thing, but you getting one? What was that about?'

'Well, you spend so much time talking about them, they're as much a part of us as they are a part of you.'

'Yeah, but you don't look out for their results or anything, do you? You can't name the current captain or the manager, or stuff like that, can you?'

She fixes him with a hard stare.

'Can we change the subject?'

An awkward silence falls upon them. They're not talking, and anyone passing would think that they were just another a tired couple at the tired end of a marriage. However, Laura's deep in thought, contemplating all that they've been through and how true happiness has passed by both of them. This knack for self-pity has always tinged her time in Australia. She has most of all she ever wanted, if not more, and an objective observer would likely mistake this malcontent for simple boredom.

'I need some time to myself,' she says eventually.

'Okay, love,' Rodney nods. 'Take care, eh?'

Wordlessly, she gets up and leaves the cafe, numb to the feeling of the floor beneath her feet.

'I'll get the bill, don't worry,' he shouts after her, a hint of sarcasm in his voice.

She doesn't bother responding.

It's a warm, bright morning, the type of which Sydney sometimes produces this time of year; the kind that makes people certain that global warming isn't just a theory but a reality. It's the middle of winter and it's twenty-four degrees; while never unheard of, it seems to be happening all too often these days, and Laura makes the most of it by wandering around past the ferries, to the steps of the Opera House. She spends some time studying the posters advertising forthcoming concerts, but she isn't really taking in much. The day may be warm, but her soul is chilled to the marrow.

She gazes up at Sydney Harbour Bridge, and it occurs to her that she's never actually done one of its famous climbs. The top, she considers, could give her a different view of the city that she calls home and perhaps offer a solution. She's been told by friends that you have to book it weeks in advance, so she resolves to call as soon as she gets back to her apartment. It seems like a very clear plan.

Try as she might, though, she can't shake off the memory of Cathy's letter. Just thinking about it pulls her away from the brightness of the day, and leaves her wallowing in the depths of sadness. She finds it impossible not to accept responsibility, and even when she finds a way to convince herself of the logic of Rodney's stance, her spirit quickly drags her back down towards a sense of guilt.

*

At this point, we should try to consider Rodney's perspective. It wasn't that he fails to understand how he could be held responsible for Cathy killing herself, but as far as he's concerned, he was merely an innocent bystander, roped into Reggie and Laura's plans as a convenient deposit for their ill-gotten gains. That's not to say that he thinks they're to blame, either. To him, there are more immediate things to feel guilty about: lovers he's hurt and those he made promises to, only to be tempted by the next bright, shiny young man that came his way. He's had a habit of treating men as disposable items, and ranked alongside that, his guilt over Cathy hardly registers on his conscience.

In his mind, Laura's being melodramatic and missing the point. He has a long-held belief that being prone to suicide is no different than being predisposed to getting fat; it's all genetic, and there's nothing you can do about it, so why worry or take responsibility? Cathy was always going to do it at some point, sure as night follows day.

There's a false narrative at play here, though, and Rodney knows it. While it's true that Cathy was uncomplicated, it's also the case that she was very sensitive. She'd been that way since she was a kid. Whenever they played games, like ludo for example, she'd get upset at losing; not because she'd been beaten, but owing to a feeling that her defeat was somehow unfair. If he really thought about it, he'd conclude that her suicide was her way of pursuing the deepest of grievances and exacting the coldest form of vengeance.

Regardless of what he does or doesn't believe, dearest reader, the bottom line is that Rodney shouldn't have shared Cathy's letter with Laura. Deep down, he knows this, and he also knows that, sadly, he'll come to regret it.

Sitting at her desk, Gertrude Millington can sense that Laura's upset about something. She's of a mind to question a couple of the points she's hearing, since during the time she's acted as Laura and Rodney's solicitor, the two women have become friends. Over the years, their relationship has developed into a kind of sisterhood, a closeness that, while not quite intimate, serves to allow them to be very relaxed in each other's company. Most importantly, they're always able to talk honestly and openly.

'Listen, Laura,' she says, peering over her reading glasses, 'if I'm being honest with you, I'm not sure that you're in a sound enough state of mind at the moment for me to accept revisions to your will.'

'I'm absolutely fine,' Laura sighs as a weak smile passes across her face. 'You worry about me too much.'

'I know you,' Gertrude says, 'and something isn't right here. You're not your usual self. I know you've been a bit down lately, so is there anything you want to share?'

A bit down! Laura thinks. *You don't know the half of it, Gertrude.*

Laura's broken. Instead of recovering from her despair, she's allowed it to envelop her, like a badly upholstered armchair that she can't get up from. There are days when she cries for two or three hours at a time, and then there are the *bad* days, when you could easily count in minutes the amount of time she *doesn't* spend crying. Whenever she reaches a stage where she thinks that her despair is lifting, she immediately sinks back down, locked into a guilty, absorbing darkness where all she can think about is how she's responsible for Cathy's death.

'Come on, Gertie,' she says gently, forcing another weak smile, 'I'm just tired. I haven't gone mad.'

Gertrude always giggles whenever Laura shortens her name.

'You sure?' she asks.

'Totally.'

Gertrude assumes her more businesslike demeanour.

'There's one sole beneficiary in the will. You sure about that?'

'Absolutely,' Laura says firmly.

'And the address given is the last known address they were at?'

Laura nods.

Gertrude sighs. 'Okay, then it's all in order. A sizeable estate like yours – people are going to be impressed with the figures.'

'I won't be around to see that,' Laura smiles.

'Oh, you'll be with us for years yet, Laura, mark my words.'

The papers are signed, and Laura stands and shakes the solicitor's hand.

'See you at the tennis club on Saturday?' Gertrude asks.

'I think so,' Laura says. 'I'll see how I am.'

As she steps out of Gertrude's office and enters the lift, Laura is, at long last, starting to experience a sense of peace. It'll be up to others to deal with the consequences of what happens next.

The doctor has arrived to assess Reggie's condition.

'Mr Kellison, you're making an excellent recovery,' he says cheerfully.

Reggie smiles, or at least he thinks it's a smile. His face muscles are contorting, he knows that much, and even though he actually looks like a dog grinning, rather than a human smiling, it still represents progress.

With maximum effort, he manages to say, 'That's... good... news.'

The doctor nods his agreement.

'It's pretty miraculous, really,' he says, 'like if Tranmere won the Champions League!'

Reggie likes Dr Jaya Rattnam. He's always kind, always courteous.

'I'd settle for promotion,' Reggie replies slowly and with huge effort.

'We don't think that you staying here's ideal, though,' Dr Rattnam says. 'You need to start doing things for yourself soon.'

Reggie's slightly worried at this. He has some of his mobility back now, but he doesn't think he's ready to go back to living alone just yet.

'Hard,' he says, hoping it sounds emphatic.

'Yes, it will be, but let's not underestimate the huge steps forward you've already taken. I don't want you becoming too institutionalised in here.'

Reggie nods, as he knows this is true. While he's grateful for the support of the physiotherapists, the speech therapist and even the cleaners, he longs to be away from Hilbre Court. He'd begun to fear that he'd been taken there to die.

'Your son has managed to find you a place to live,' Dr Rattnam says. 'Woodchurch Court. It's in Oxton.'

'Posh,' Reggie remarks.

'It's better than posh,' the doctor says warmly, 'it's walking distance from Prenton Park!'

Reggie chuckles, and as he does so, a tear runs down his cheek.

'Happy,' he says, wiping it away.

'Excellent. It's semi-sheltered accommodation, warden-assisted. We should be able to move you in the next few weeks.'

Reggie's determined to get the next sentence out in full.

'Before…' He pauses for breath and tries again. 'Before the start of the new season!'

'Absolutely,' Dr Rattnam grins. 'Yes, in time for the first game, I'd imagine.'

Later, lying awake in his bed, Reggie ponders recent events. He'd never have chosen for his life to go this way; he hates his lack of mobility, his confinement within a body that no longer feels like his own, and being unable to do the things that he'd previously taken for granted. Yet, this is still life, and he's still breathing. This is a future, even if it's not the one he'd imagined.

On the other side of the world, Laura's mood doesn't match Reggie's.

It's Saturday morning, drizzly rain is falling, and the absence of any breeze suggests that the weather is in for the day. This is disappointing, as she'd been hoping for a bright, clear afternoon. She's worried that the rain will mean that her bridge climb will be cancelled, but when she checks online, she's relieved to find that it's due to go ahead as planned.

She showers, eats breakfast in her dressing gown, and then puts on a pair of jeans, a sweatshirt and some trainers, in accordance with what the website advised. She tidies away her breakfast plates, placing them in the dishwasher. There aren't enough of them for a full load, but she hates to leave a mess.

Closing the door behind her, she starts to feel lighter. A sense of relief grows within her, until it becomes something approaching euphoria as she arrives at The Rocks in a taxi. She tips the driver generously, handing him a fifty-dollar note with instructions to keep the change.

'You sure?' he asks. 'I mean, it's only a nine-dollar fare.'

She nods, and the bemused driver would later explain that he didn't really clock where he was dropping her, as his mind was focused on the England vs Australia test match on the radio.

She's taken through the safety procedures and then given a garish blue boiler suit to wear, which makes everyone taking part look like a prison inmate. The atmosphere is jolly, though. It reminds her of being on a school outing. As the final preparations are made, she places a note on top of her belongings and closes her locker. It's addressed to Rodney.

The climb itself isn't so scary, and she wonders if the emphasis on safety is just part of the hype, to make people think that they're doing something riskier than they actually are. The only challenging part is getting up the little steel ladder that takes you to the start of the upper-bridge span. *Going down might be harder,* she thinks, *since people will be tired by then.*

The view is magnificent. Even on this grey day, she can see all around the harbour, across to Bondi Beach and over to Manly. She's reminded why she's always loved this city.

Hanging back from her group, she unclips her safety harness, says a short prayer and then jumps.

The last thing she hears is the screaming of the other members in her climbing group, and as she leaves the bridge, falling, twisting and seeing the water rising rapidly to meet her, her final conscious thoughts are of Cathy's letter.

I forgot to put it away, she realises. *It's still out on the dressing table.*

This makes her feel very guilty.

Rodney had spent his Saturday afternoon in the sauna, and he has no plans for the evening outside of watching some football and listening to music. As he enters his apartment building, still thinking about the Malaysian teen he'd encountered earlier in the day, he's accosted by the concierge.

'Rodney,' he hears, 'the police are looking for you!'

It's just the sort of joke that Kelvin is prone to cracking. Rodney reckons that the concierge knows about his sexuality, and that most of the comments he makes are his way of joshing.

'Oh aye,' Rodney smiles, 'do they think I'm Ronnie Biggs now?'

'No, mate,' Kelvin says firmly, 'I'm being serious. There's been some sort of accident involving your ex-wife.'

He hands Rodney a business card containing contact details for a detective in the local police department.

'Right, right,' Rodney says calmly.

This detail would also be mentioned during the inquest – how he seemed incredibly calm about everything that happened.

He takes the lift up to his apartment, and once inside, grabs his mobile phone and dials the number on the business card. After explaining who he is, he's put through to a desk sergeant.

'Ah, Mr Yardley,' the officer says, 'we need you to come and see us as soon as possible. There's been a terrible incident involving your ex-wife. Can you come to the station, please?'

'Now?'

'I'm afraid so, sir, yes. We think she might have killed herself. She left a note behind in her locker. It's addressed to you.'

'Her locker?' Rodney asks, wondering why Laura would have such a thing.

'We'll explain everything in full once you've arrived. Please come as soon as you can, sir.'

Rodney hangs up. He paces the flat for a moment and then pours himself a glass of whisky. He goes to down it in one gulp but spits it back out after realising that, given the circumstances, he needs to keep his wits about him.

The next seven or eight hours are the longest of his life. It feels like the sky's caving in while the earth swallows him whole. It feels like the end of the world.

The fixtures are out! David cheers internally after his idle web surfing takes him to a football news site. It's a bright July morning, and the warmth makes him think back to Sydney. He really enjoyed his time there. He loved the sense of freedom it offered, and how the people weren't shackled by the stuffiness that permeates through the UK.

His favourite Australian pastime had been morning coffee down at The Rocks. He'd leaf through the *Sydney Morning Herald*, a great read, and just enjoy the world passing by. Subsequently, he now regularly visits their website, finding that while it isn't quite the same experience, it's still a good read. Opening the *Herald*'s home page, his eye is drawn to a headline in the Local News section.

'Inquest Opens into Sydney Harbour Bridge Climb Suicide', he reads.

He'd done the bridge climb himself and had really enjoyed it. While he'd been up there doing it, the thought had occurred to him that what was sold as a 'thrill' was, in reality, quite tame. A name jumps out at him as he reads on.

The coroner will today open an investigation into the death of Laura Yardley, who threw herself from the Harbour Bridge early last month.

Surely not, he thinks.

Ms Yardley, of Darlinghurst Harbour, is believed to have taken her own life...

He feels the panic rising. *What is this?*

It's 8.30a.m., and he picks up his mobile and calls Barry.

'Rovers not playing today, David?' is his brother's light-hearted greeting.

'Baz, I've just read something shocking!' David says and then reads the article out in full.

'Fucking hell,' Barry mutters under his breath.

This is very uncharacteristic. He very rarely swears, even when the referee is the most useless donkey you've ever come across.

'Have you contacted Rodney?'

'Not yet, no. I've only just seen it.'

There's a heavily pregnant silence.

'Don't tell Dad,' Barry says. 'Not yet, anyway. You know how upset he gets, and we don't want something like this making him ill again.'

'He'll have to find out at some point, though, yeah?'

'Why? He's never going to see or hear from her again, so why does he have to know?'

Dear reader, you can now see the difference between Barry and his uncle Rodney. Barry understands that information is currency, with a value that can harm. If only Rodney had known this. David, however, isn't comfortable with Barry's decision. He knows that his dad will be upset by this, but that he'll feel even worse if he hears that they knew and didn't tell him.

David agrees to contact Rodney, who he figures must also be feeling upset over what has happened. He dials his uncle's mobile number, but all he gets is a message saying, 'It has not been possible to connect your call.'

He begins to worry.

Rodney had met with the police on several occasions after Laura took her own life. This included the initial session at the mortuary, where he formally identified her body, and was followed by multiple interviews regarding the circumstances of her death. The questions were always the same:

'Was there any hint that she was planning this?'

'How would you describe her state of mind?'

And so on…

It was only during what would prove to be the final interview, after the police had searched Laura's flat, that the matter of Cathy's letter had emerged.

'Why did she have a letter from your sister in her apartment, which was addressed to you?'

Rodney had been getting increasingly more concerned since that last interview, as the letter not only referred to his sexuality, but also hinted at past crimes. He was worried that the police would start digging into where his wealth came from, and where that could possibly lead them.

Dear reader, we have, have we not, seen Rodney as a loveable rogue? He's a man who drives without a licence, risks danger

193

and explores sexual opportunities in what we might call a predatory way. He's a clever chap, or is he? What if he's not so much a loveable rogue as he's simply a scoundrel? Is our opinion of him changing?

'That letter,' Rodney had explained, 'do you know, she stole it from me!'

He then concocted a long explanation, detailing how, when he got back from England, Laura had visited his apartment and helped him to unpack.

Of course, none of what he claimed actually happened, and especially not the part where she found the letter and demanded to read it. Just as false was his assertion that she seemed indifferent to the contents of the letter, but the only thing the police had to go on was Rodney's word, along with his exaggerated pain at the loss of his ex-wife. He's always been a gifted liar, and he knows how to be a rogue when it suits him. Laura's no longer around to give evidence, so all he needs to do is keep everything plausible.

The police officers displayed little concern for Rodney's sexuality, and even less about the cryptic references to his past life in England. All they wanted was to be able to close the case and present their report to the coroner. As it happens, Mr Justice Whitby mentioned in passing that it was unfortunate that her ex-husband had inadvertently allowed her to see some distressing correspondence he'd received from his deceased sister. However, he was convinced that this was not, in and of itself, relevant to Mrs Yardley taking her own life. Therefore, the verdict, recorded by the inquest, was death by way of suicide.

Rodney didn't have to give direct evidence in the inquest. That was left to a host of others, including a taxi driver, other tourists up on the bridge climb that day and safety managers from the BridgeClimb company. At its conclusion, Rodney didn't hang around. It was a grim nod of thanks to the coroner and then out via a rear door, avoiding any contact with the handful of local reporters assigned to the story.

Was it justice? Sadly not. Redemption? Again, no. Relief? Yes, relief of sorts, and a lingering sense that he needed to leave Australia. He needed to disappear.

'This is alright this, Reggie,' Fred enthuses, admiring his friend's new flat. 'You've got everything you need here, eh?'

Reggie nods enthusiastically. It's a nice little place, no palace by any means but more than adequate, with a neat little lounge, a small kitchen and a decent-sized bedroom. The bathroom could be bigger, but it isn't what you'd call pokey. It's Woodchurch Court.

'Are the neighbours nice?' Fred asks, keen and enthusiastic as always.

'Lovely,' Reggie says with some effort.

Speech still isn't easy, but nor is it impossible. He can now string together whole sentences when he puts his mind to it; though with Fred or the family, there isn't much need for that. Fred and he have known each other for so long, there's no obligation to fill a silent space with chit-chat.

David enters, carrying Reggie's post.

'Mostly just bills, Dad,' he says, a touch of despondency in his voice.

Reggie pulls a face of mock horror, which draws a laugh from his son.

'There's this, though,' David says, holding up an embossed envelope from Millington & Partners, marked with Australian stamps.

It had been forwarded on a redirection notice from Hilbre Court.

'Aussie pools?' Fred chuckles.

Reggie looks at the envelope curiously.

'Give,' he says gently, politely.

'Do you want me to open it for you?' David asks.

'Give,' Reggie says more firmly, shaking his head.

He places the envelope on his lap for a moment, uncertain, and then studies it.

'Go on,' Fred says, 'open it.'

'Please?' Reggie replies, looking at Fred.

'You want *me* to?' Fred gestures towards the envelope.

'Yes,' Reggie says.

Fred opens the envelope and passes its contents to Reggie, who reads it twice.

'Fucking hell,' he says.

'What?' David asks. 'Are you having a relapse?'

'Read,' he says to David, rubbing tears from his eyes.

'Dear Mr Kellison,' David reads aloud, 'I am sorry to inform you that Ms Laura Yardley, known to you as Laura Biggs, recently passed away.' He glances up at his father, obviously worried about what this could do to him. 'I'm sorry, Dad.'

'Read!' Reggie insists.

David continues. 'Laura has left her entire estate to you. This is of considerable value, approximately £2.5 million, plus her apartment in Darlinghurst Harbour, as well as some other personal belongings.'

It's now Fred's turn to swear.

'Fucking hell, Reggie, that's bigger than any Aussie payout!'

David's now reading with excitement in his voice.

'I would be grateful if you could arrange for your legal representatives to contact me directly, in order that we can arrange for this matter to be resolved.'

He screams a joyous scream.

'Shush!' Reggie chides him. 'Laura's dead,' he says forlornly.

David places his hand on top of his dad's and squeezes.

'I'm sorry, Pops,' he says gently.

'Don't you "Sorry, Pops" him, lad,' Fred interrupts. 'You're a fucking millionaire, Reggie!'

'Not the point,' Reggie says quietly. 'No Laura.'

The room falls silent until finally Reggie says, 'Five minutes?'

'What?' David asks.

'Five minutes, me, alone. Please?'

Fred and David respect his wishes and walk down to the large communal lounge.

Left alone with his thoughts, all Reggie can do is think of Laura. Her hair, her voice and now her kindness. *She didn't need to do this,* he thinks. He would, he knew, have preferred to see her. That would have been worth more than a planeload of money from the other side of the world.

Reader, we don't always get what we want. We aren't always allowed to choose our gifts, or how our good fortune is delivered. Embossed envelopes bring both good and bad news. We can celebrate Reggie's good fortune, and even raise our glasses to it, yet his overwhelming sense is of loss and sadness. The joy will come later, but the sadness will never leave.

Fred eventually pops his head around the door.

'You OK?' he asks.

Reggie nods.

'Come on, then,' Fred says.

'What?' Reggie asks.

'We're not sitting here with you being all maudlin. Me and your David are taking you round to the Shrew. You can drown your sorrows, and I, for the first time in me life, can buy a multimillionaire a pint. Plus, you don't have to be nice to that witch of a Tory landlady. Get your coat!'

At around about the same time that the post arrives in Woodchurch Court, Rodney's stepping off a plane in Bangkok. It's a hot day, but still the rain falls from the sky, and then falls some more. He's here for a few weeks, with no firm plans. He's sold up in Sydney. Everything is gone now. All he has left are the clothes in his two suitcases and a fortune in the bank. He has a vague notion of a plan to stay in Bangkok for a few days and then head down to Koh Samui. There, he'll find a place to rent, and he also fancies getting himself a young houseboy who'll apply himself to more than just his domestic needs. At the same time, and this comes as a shock to him, he's getting bored of the constant pursuit of new conquests, as he finds that it isn't as fulfilling as it used to be. It's like porn, in that after a while, too much exposure removes the thrill. He's losing his drive.

He's slightly depressed by this. Now into his late sixties, although he passes for a much younger man, it seems odd not to need to touch somebody else constantly, or to have somebody touch him. He's confused about what this means. *Am I past it?* he wonders.

The absence of sexual pursuits means that he doesn't quite enjoy Bangkok in the way he'd expected. It appears that once you take away the sex, all that remains is a seedy, loud city with good food and poor air conditioning. *I could be anywhere in South East Asia,* he realises. Kuala Lumpur, Singapore, Bangkok – they all look like copies of one another, and it feels as though nothing in these gleaming metropolises will last much longer than it takes to consume a bowl of rice. Chiang Mai is better, but even there he feels disassociated and disconnected from the world around him.

Things improve when he reaches Koh Samui. He giggles at the Fisher Price-like qualities of the airport, as if designed by a team of four-year-olds, and then heads to Bophut, with its long beach, trendy restaurants and nightlife at Fisherman's Village. After a few days, he already feels like a local, having found an apartment with a pool and started trying to learn Thai. He'll soon become *Lodney* the Local, and spend his days chatting to all and sundry while, quite unexpectedly, becoming somewhat asexual.

Does he miss Australia? The question isn't relevant, as he lives only in the present moment. He follows Tranmere's results online and occasionally thinks about flying out to catch a late-season game or an August kick-off. When it comes down to it, though, England just makes him grimace. In Bophut, he's the life and soul of the party. Back home, he'd just be some old guy, balding and shouting at referees, with nothing interesting to say.

You'll agree that this isn't a bad life for Rodney, but nor, I suspect, is it a life you'd want for yourself.

Many people say that money won't change them. This is a mantra that Reggie had often thought would apply to him. He can't drive, so he doesn't need a car. He has all he wants at Woodchurch Court, and although travel had appealed to his younger self, he knows that his choices are limited post-stroke.

'Don't you want to leave this place?' Fred often asks.

Reggie always gives the same response.

'Happy,' he says. 'No point. Nice people, nice flat. Moving would be a waste of money.'

His speech has become quicker, albeit still staccato. He speaks like an automated voice reading a text message now, with his face – and let's face it, this should be true of everyone – serving as his emoji.

He uses his wealth to good effect, buying houses for all of his kids, or else paying off existing mortgages. This makes him happy, but he's still only used up a quarter of his inheritance from Laura. He resists the temptation to put money into Tranmere Rovers, despite David being really keen on the idea.

At the start of the season, which follows his becoming a wealthy man, Reggie, Fred, Barry and David meet in the Halfway House before the opening game; two quite old men with their middle-aged minders.

'What do you reckon, then, Reggie? Easy win today?' Fred asks.

'Tranmere,' Reggie says. 'Nothing ever easy!'

'You're dead right there, Dad,' David chuckles.

'We need to get off to a good start,' Barry chimes in. 'Get a few points on the board, and avoid spending the season looking over our shoulders.'

Reggie listens. He nods in the right places and glances at the door occasionally, half expecting to see someone he knows. He imagines Laura walking in, and smiling and waving when she sees him.

'You wasting your inheritance on this lot?' she'd say teasingly, and he'd just smile, basking in her beauty and adoring her jibes.

It's just a shame that it's never going to happen.

At 2.45p.m., they make the short walk down Woodchurch Lane.

'Dad,' David says.

'Yes?' Reggie answers.

'I've got this new song that I want to teach you and Fred, OK? It's to the tune of "When the Saints Go Marching In".'

'Go on.'

'OK, sing it after me... Oh Birkenhead,' he half sings.

Reggie and Fred repeat the line.

'Is wonderful!'

Again, they join in.

'Oh Birkenhead is wonderful… It's full of tits and Tranmere Rovers—'

'Rude!' Reggie laughs.

'Go on, Dad,' David encourages, 'it's ace!'

They sing the song a couple of times as they march down Woodchurch Lane, with Reggie and Fred chuckling at the rudeness, and Barry and David enjoying their discomfort.

*

There, dear reader, we must leave them. There are, truth be told, other local attractions to visit on a warm Saturday afternoon. What are they? Well, there's New Brighton or West Kirby, if you want refinement. You could even go to Woodside and take the ferry across the Mersey, with its endless repetition of the song it inspired. Yet, for these four men, and the several thousand with them, the dream and allure of Prenton Park, the hope that springs eternal in the wind and the rain, is all that matters, and all that can ever make them happy.

Our tale is done.

EPILOGUE

For months, he's been sitting in a darkened room. His speech has gone completely now, along with his mobility – nine years after the first attack, the stroke has returned with a vengeance. It's been a few years since Fred passed away, and life has become distinctly lonely. He's back in a nursing home, albeit a posh one this time, Mount Pleasant House, in Oxton. Sometimes, if he strains his ears, Reggie can hear the roar of the crowd at Prenton Park.

Only David comes to see him now, once a week, on a Sunday. Despite having lost the power of speech, he hasn't lost interest in the world, and David seems to sense this. He provides his dad with updates on Tranmere, politics and life in general, but Reggie, no matter how he tries, can't converse with him. He can, however, move his right index finger, but nobody seems to have noticed.

Sometimes, when David's there, he tries to tap out Rovers songs, and after several months, the rhythm is finally recognised. David even joins in, singing through the tears.

'It's full of tits and Tranmere Rovers,' he sings along, laughing and crying in equal measure.

Yet, no amount of singing can disguise the truth that Reggie is on his way out.

He tries a new song on David, but he doesn't notice for ages, until finally, when almost all of his strength has gone, it gets through.

He counts out the rhythm first:

'Dah-dah-dah-dah-dah-dah,   dah-dah-dah-dah-dah-dah, dah-dah-dah-dah, dah-dah-dah-dah, dah-dah-dah-dah-dah-dah...'

Then David picks up the words.

'I'm Tranmere till I die, I'm Tranmere till I die, I know I am, I'm sure I am, I'm Tranmere till I die!'

They both cry, one old man and one man in early middle age, on a cold Sunday in October.

Over the course of the following week, Tranmere will lose two games, one in the League Cup and another away at Crewe, and on the Saturday evening they'll lose Reggie. An imperfect life, but a perfect man and a perfect fan.

Now this tale really is done.

TRUTH OR FICTION?
THE BACKGROUND TO PLAYING THE POOLS

Thank you for reading *Playing the Pools*.

The novel is a work of fiction based upon facts. My dad worked at Littlewoods Pools in Liverpool in the 1960s and then went on to work as a ticket collector at the Woodside Terminus of the Mersey Ferries. He, like me, was a fanatical Tranmere Rovers supporter, which just proves that madness is hereditary. My dad also had a stroke when he was forty-eight, and some of the details of his experience are covered later in the book. However, he didn't end up in a nursing home. Instead my mum looked after him and supported him until he died when I was seventeen.

Sometime around about 1974, after his stroke, my dad submitted an idea for a summer cricket pool to Littlewoods. This was rejected, but the following summer Littlewoods launched a coupon very similar to my dad's idea. Whilst I am not implying that the idea was stolen, I was able to bring the fact that my dad worked at Littlewoods together with the cricket pool idea to create a motive. However, Reggie's work colleagues are all fictitious, including Laura. The exception is Fred Hughes. He was one of my dad's closest mates and they worked together as bus crew, in Birkenhead, and at the Ferries. To my knowledge Fred never had a job at Littlewoods.

After Dad had his stroke, I spent a great deal of time with him. Being the youngest of six, with a gap of more than five years between me and my sister Kay, meant that after she had gone to university, I was left at home. Dad and I would chat about everything. This included politics, Tranmere, his memories of Birkenhead from his childhood and so much more. He cemented my love for Tranmere as, after his stroke, he was rarely able to get to the games. I would rush home to give him a report on our win, or, as more often was the case, our defeat. (Fittingly, the evening he died, I watched Tranmere v Cambridge United, as I was at a loss as to what else to do.)

Uncle Rodney was not my mum's brother but my dad's. He emigrated to Canada around about 1962. One of my earliest memories is from December 1961, when he changed a light bulb in our hall. I was eleven months old, but the mind plays tricks, and I am no longer sure if this is a true memory. Rodney died in London, Ontario, Canada. He was a fine and upstanding member of his local community, but I never saw him again.

Many of the places mentioned in the novel exist. The Halfway House is a well-known pub about quarter of a mile from Prenton Park. I can often be found in there before games enjoying a convivial pint before a match. Some of the places no longer exist, such as the Woodside Hotel, but they did at one point.

Finally, I should acknowledge all the help I have had in putting together this book. My eldest brother Barry, Tranmere Rovers supporters themselves via the Cowshed website, numerous friends who read early drafts and the team at RedDoor, who have been a delight to work with. Special thanks go to Heather Boisseau, who has guided, supported, and encouraged me during the production process.

David M Sindall, West Kirby, 2021

ABOUT THE AUTHOR

David Sindall lives in West Kirby on the Wirral. He grew up in Birkenhead and spent most of his career working in the field of diversity.

Playing the Pools is his third novel following on from *After Alyson* (2012) and *Snatched* (2016).

DAVID M. SINDALL

SNATCHED

Kieran
Berlin
April 17th
15:40

Many people would probably despise what I do for a living. I don't care. No job is morally neutral. Priests absolve people of disgusting things; nurses take part in abortions; firefighters call in sick. People ignore all of that shit so they can feel better about their own lives. Think about what you do each day and ask yourself do you really make a living in such a pure way? I'm pretty sure that when you think about it, there's a deal you know about that you want to keep quiet, something you would rather not mention over a beer with your buddies. The guy who got fired who you didn't stand up for, the expenses claim that was a bit iffy, the elected official who is suspect, but you keep quiet about. I know that you know. You just don't want to be honest with yourself.

I can sleep soundly at night and I make good money. I pay all my taxes; I even vote for progressive parties of the centre left. Last year I gave over 200K to children's charities and not as some poxy tax loophole on the advice of my accountant. I always tip well too, just as the waitress who is approaching my table knows.

She says something to me that I pretend I don't understand.

'English,' I say and she smiles.

'Would you like another beer?' she says, as the smile lingers on her face.

'*Ja*,' I say, 'but you'll have to fill in the rest for yourself because I don't speak German.'

This is a lie, but it's a useful lie. I speak reasonable German; it just suits my purpose that people think I am a clumsy English businessman.

'Hey, no worries,' she says, flashing me a perfect smile. 'I like to speak English. You here for long?'

'Unfortunately not,' I say. 'I have a meeting in London tomorrow.'

'You'll need to get to Tegel then?'

I shake my head, showing disagreement.

'I hate flying. Why fly when you have *Deutsche Bahn*?'

She looks at me, interested. I know that look. If I were staying in Berlin tonight I reckon I could meet her later, buy her dinner and end up back at her place. Another time.

She smiles. 'Back soon, with your beer, OK?'

I let her go, it is pointless flirting with her and I want time to reflect.

I look across to the Reichstag. I love the building – the shape of it and the sense of it being a phoenix rising from the ashes. A city divided is a city united. Berlin has everything. Great people, great buildings and an amazing history. What's not to like? My clients like it here too. They can blend in, they don't get too much attention and they can come here without raising suspicion.

In my job, blending in is important. I am never rude and never overfamiliar with people. I do nothing to draw attention to myself. You've got to be a bit of a prick not to blend in, so the first rule is not to do anything that makes you seem difficult, showy or memorable in anyway whatsoever. I dress business casual. Not Armani or anything flash, just Marks and Spencer. If I wear jeans they're Levi's; my watch is cheap – not a Rolex, my phone and my laptop are never the latest kit. I just have a way of presenting myself that says, 'nothing memorable'.

Sometimes my clients are initially shocked. The deal I

closed this morning was worth twelve million euros. I think some of the people I work for would be happier if I arrived in a Porsche and big Prada shades, looking like some movie star. If I did, I could guarantee every fucker everywhere would notice me. I don't want to be noticed. This extends to everything else too. I have a modest house in St. Albans. I have another apartment in central London, but my neighbours there think I'm an IT specialist, renting on a company let. The only luxury I afford myself is occasional First class ticket on Eurostar. Everything else about me is inoffensive and understated. There is one exception – I have a place in Biarritz. A project I started about five years ago, an old, enormous château. Rooms everywhere. It is my hideaway, my refuge and the nearest I have to a real base. Yet the chateau is so private I don't have to worry. The one thing I like about the French – and let's face it with their arrogant wines, snotty waiters and useless cars there isn't much to actually like – is that they respect your privacy, they keep their distance.

The waitress brings my beer back. In a few weeks' time I will be drinking in Rome, meeting my client from this morning at the Champions League final. We will have good seats; it will fit with the deception of my job. Officially, I run a ticket agency where I specialise in hard to get sports tickets. Mostly in Europe, but, sometimes, particularly if the client is North American, it might be cricket in the Caribbean or basketball in NYC. The important thing is that the deception is maintained. We'll go through the whole charade. Go to the match together, be seen enjoying each other's company, so that the story absolutely fits. Luckily, it's football, so I might enjoy it. If it were rugby or, God forbid, golf, I'd be in for a tedious 'day at the office'. Then, at the end of the match, he'll go back to Moscow, I'll take a train to London and life will go on. The deal isn't due for completion until the group stages of next year's competition. Doubtless, we will end up in the Nou Camp to sort out the final details. I look after my clients, there'll be no complications.

If people knew what I did, I suspect they'd wonder how I got in to this line of work. I wish I had a complex answer, but there isn't much to explain. I'm the son of a London Underground ticket collector. I did a degree in Psychology and specialised in Child Psychology. Unlike all the other losers who ended up in the public sector, I wanted to make some real money. To begin with, though, I never knew how, I stumbled on this lark when I was reading the colour supplements one Sunday. The rest is history, albeit not very nice history.

Time is passing. I am twenty minutes from the Hauptbahnhof. I need to get Anna moving back in London.

Find out more about RedDoor
Press and sign up to our
newsletter to hear about our
latest releases, author events,
exciting **competitions**
and more at

reddoorpress.co.uk

YOU CAN ALSO FOLLOW US:

 @RedDoorBooks

 Facebook.com/RedDoorPress

 @RedDoorBooks